BOJI

THE BLUE DOLPHIN

Robert Barnes

Boji

THE
BLUE
DOLPHIN

A story by

ROBERT BARNES

ISBN 0 9518166 0 8

Cover design by Lawrence Edwards
Cover photograph by Robert Barnes
Typesetting by Postscript Publishing Services, No. 1 Argyle
Street, Bath BA2 4BA
Printed in Great Britain by The Cromwell Press, Broughton
Gifford, Melksham, Wiltshire SN12 8PH

To the dolphin energy

that dwells in us all

ONE

The surface of the sea heaved gently, reflecting the steady gold of the early morning sun.

Within a few hundred metres low cliffs dived steeply into the deep blue-green water.

Beneath the swell a pod of eight bottlenose dolphins was engaged in finding breakfast. This particular morning it seemed the sea was reluctant to give of its bounty. An area normally well populated with their prey fish was almost devoid of any life larger than the larval stage.

The dolphins spread out, and using blasts of subtle sound generated and directed from within their smooth heads, relied on the returning echoes to tell them where the first meal of the day might be found.

Of the five adult females in the pod, Nevina was the youngest and still getting used to her maturity and acceptance as an equal by her four elders. From a joyful encounter with another pod four months before she knew she was carrying her first calf. Aware of a growing presence within her, she enjoyed the new dimension her pregnancy added to her life.

Nevina had known from the start that her calf was male, the quality of the energy which had added itself to hers was quite distinct. What she did not know yet was a name for him, but she was confident one would come to her as soon as he was born.

Right now she was hungry, and her hunger dominated her actions. Swimming parallel to the coastline she sent out sonar signals ahead, with little or no result. The sea was strangely empty.

A fast, high pitched collection of sounds reached out to Nevina from further out to sea. She recognised the acoustic signature of Tanya, one of the older females, followed by the clear image in sound of the echoes normally created by one of the pod's favourite prey fish. Nevina transmitted her own sound signature in response and swam after it. She heard the other members of the pod similarly homing in on Tanya.

After a swim which took her way beyond their normal feeding grounds, Nevina drew close to Tanya. She detected the fish herself, but they were behaving oddly. Some were moving erratically and in one spot, others were very still in mid-water.

Tanya, having waited until the rest of the pod were near, plunged toward a large fish moving normally through the water several metres beyond the stationary ones. Joliba, her year old calf, swam close alongside her in excited anticipation of satisfying his hunger.

Their progress through the water was arrested abruptly. Tanya tried to drive onward and felt many thin cutting edges biting into her fins and tail flukes. Turning to escape this threat she was enveloped in netting so fine it had been invisible to her in the dark waters and undetected by her sonar.

In staying close to his mother, Joliba suffered the same fate. There was a moment of hesitation when he could have backed away and remained free of the deadly net, but seeing his mother in distress he moved toward her - and became hopelessly enmeshed himself within a metre of her.

They called to each other, filling the water with their sound signatures. They tried to move closer together, to touch each other again. Such efforts only entangled them tighter into the fine but very strong netting, and they stayed a metre apart.

Nevina and the rest of the pod were now gathered and still. Against the light background of Tanya's and Joliba's bodies they could at least now see the problem. The fine lines of the monofilament net were clearly visible, enveloping and holding their fellows in what would be inevitably their last few minutes of life. The surface was tantalisingly close, no more than five or six metres above them - but it might as well have been a hundred. They were held fast, and the life giving air for the next breath was beyond their reach.

Seeing the frustration and the desperation of the trapped mother and calf brought horrific visions to Nevina's imagination. Soon she would have a calf of her own, and within a year she could be in the same position as Tanya - dying, and unable to protect or save her calf from the fine netting which could not be detected until it was too late.

Her visions brought fear and revulsion in their wake. The feelings coursed through her body and her calf was immersed in them, contracting sharply in a hopeless attempt to avoid them. He felt contaminated.

Nevina and the rest of the pod were powerless. After several minutes of communicating messages of love and encouragement they fell silent. Their sonar images of Tanya and Joliba were telling them of the need for air and the changes the lack of it was causing within their bodies. Normally, the healthy dolphins would attempt to lift ailing companions to the surface, but Tanya had screamed at them to keep away, sending images of the inevitable result - more of them becoming trapped.

Joliba died first, and the water was full of Tanya's grief. Sadness cloaked Nevina and the rest of the pod. Her calf within was overcome by the weight of his mother's feelings. The power and intensity of emotion within a short space of time felt overwhelming. Until now he had experienced nothing but delight at the warmth and love of his mother's body. These new and powerful emotions presented a threat,

3

an unknown quality which coloured his vulnerability, his perception of life and himself from that time forward.

Without life giving oxygen, Tanya's body closed down until only the vital organs remained alive. Then, one by one they ceased to function until, finally, death came to her. Having no breathing reflex she could choose to breathe or not. As the air was not available to her she did what she was used to doing underwater - she simply held her breath and the end came by suffocation, not by drowning.

In farewell, the rest of the pod lovingly transmitted Tanya's and Joliba's sound signatures for the last time at the bodies of their former companions, followed by their own, and then moved away in silence toward the distant shore.

Nevina stayed with the pod for a while, and then slowed to a halt. Her sadness was coloured by a desire to know more about the drifting nets which brought death to all but the smallest creatures of the sea. The more she knew the better she could guide and protect her calf from the same fate as Joliba.

She transmitted sound images of herself in good health to the rest of the pod to reassure them. The remaining three mature females and two young male offspring continued on their way.

Recognising now the line of the drifting net by the presence of fish held in strange attitudes in the water, and by the bodies of her former companions, Nevina kept her distance and waited. She knew there was a risk of sharks being attracted to the dead and struggling life in the net, but she had to know what was to become of the net and its contents.

At intervals Nevina turned through a full circle, sending her deeper sonar frequencies out into the ocean to give her early warning of any distant, unfamiliar echoes. She did not have to wait long. The morning was only an hour or so older when a shape appeared at the surface coming toward her. She had detected many like it before. It was the underside of a human vehicle accompanied by propeller sounds.

As the fishing boat came closer and slowed, Nevina spy-hopped. Hanging vertically in the water with her head above the surface, she waited to see what the humans would do.

Moving past her, the drift net boat followed the line of floats which marked the top of the net. From above the water Nevina could see the end of the floats some four hundred metres from her in the direction of the distant shore, barely visible on the horizon. Following them the other way, the floats disappeared into the distance in a long wavering line.

The boat had come to a halt at the end of the net. The humans appeared on board in a welter of noise and movement. The clank of machinery started and after a few moments the net began to appear above water. Fifteen metres deep from floats to lead-cored foot rope, the net narrowed and folded as it was hauled upward,easily visible now against the hull of the fishing boat.

Nevina watched, fascinated. She recognised so many different creatures familiar to her. Varieties of fish which were good to eat, others which were neither prey nor predator, the occasional shark. A turtle, still struggling, was hauled up, clattering against the side of the boat. She saw seabirds caught in the top metre or so of net. They were thrown back into the sea quite dead - as were some of the fish which were presumably of no interest to the humans.

After about ten minutes of this grisly activity, the bodies of Tanya and Joliba emerged from the water. At the sight of them, Nevina felt the pain of separation well up again and once more her calf reacted to protect himself against the brief inflow of his mother's hurt.

The dead dolphins, held by the net, were hauled up and out of sight on to the boat's deck. Within moments they were thrown back into the sea to sink slowly downward.

Nevina was in shock and totally confused. Tanya and Joliba had been killed - for what? The humans clearly did not want them any more than they wanted the seabirds or the pieces of driftwood which were similarly thrown overboard as waste. These upright bipeds, which she had seen on their boats, albeit rarely, had not been a threat to her until now. She felt no enmity toward them, she wasn't capable of such a reaction. They had been simply another presence in her world and, until now, a non-interfering one. That had changed. Perhaps these humans should be bracketed with sharks and other predators in her mind as a life form to be wary of in future.

The experience had left its mark on Nevina and her developing calf. Shaken and subdued, she turned away from the carnage she had witnessed, making for the distant shoreline and the welcome support of the remaining five dolphins in her home pod.

TWO

Several months passed.

The seasons had changed and conditions at the surface, and for several metres down, were noticeably warmer.

Since the loss of Tanya and her calf, the life of home pod had been uneventful. The dolphins had moved along the coast to change their habitual feeding grounds and the sea was surrendering its abundance for their survival once again.

What did affect Nevina was the occasional appearance of one of the humans' boats. She found herself diving deep when the shape of a hull became clear, and her fear kept her down as long as she could, surfacing only when she had to, well away from the alien presence.

One particular morning, Nevina was delighted that the sea was in mellow mood. She knew she was close to giving birth to her calf, and had to be near to the surface when he emerged for his first breath. The easy swell was perfect, and she was grateful for the warmth in the upper layers of water.

Her companions had kept track of her growing calf, checking on him with their sonar, and then reporting to her what they had perceived. They assured her constantly that the small body within her own was developing perfectly. And yet Nevina felt uneasy. Each time she had experienced strong emotions during her pregnancy, particularly the sadness and the fear, she had felt her calf react strongly, the difference and power of his movements were unmistakeably out of the norm. She just hoped he had also felt her times of intense joy, love and contentment during their time together.

Now she had located a small area of water a few degrees warmer than the surrounding ocean and she drifted with it.

For some weeks she had been creating in her mind pictures of how she wanted the birth to be, seeing herself in calm, clear water with her friends in the pod close by if needed. As she had grown to maturity she had witnessed many births so she had a good idea of what was to come.

Nevina propelled herself to the surface to take another breath, the blowhole on top of her smooth, rounded head opening and closing again in half a second. As she rolled back into a shallow swimming depth her forward motion was arrested abruptly and she felt minute lines of pressure over her head and fins. Several vertical filaments scraped quickly across her eyes now closed in pain and awful realisation.

No! No! Not this! Not now!

She had not seen anything to reveal the drifting, discarded portion of fine netting. There were no floats, no weighted rope, as yet no fish in strange attitudes, no need for her to use her sonar. She must have been the first to encounter this unwanted section of the humans' drift nets.

At first she kept very still, sensing, feeling where the net touched her body. Only her tail flukes were still clear, the fine squares of monofilament nylon had closed around her from the head backwards. Gently she tested the possibility of reverse movement, but her flippers and dorsal fin were held fast.

Could she get to the surface? She was very close, only about a metre down. She reached upward and thrust hard with her tail - yes! The top of her head, enclosed by only one layer of net, broke the surface and she took three quick breaths in her stress.

Nevina was flooded with fear - not for herself so much as her calf. Images flashed through her mind of him being born straight into the folds of the net. He would die before he had a chance to live!

For his part her calf's body burned as his mother's fear flowed into him through the umbilical cord. He fought against it, but was powerless to stop it filling his body. He was fully developed and ready for birth. The space available to him, once open and welcoming, now felt cramped, restricting and increasingly threatening. He knew instinctively that he had to move, to go somewhere, but he didn't know where. He directed thoughts at his mother.

'What's happening? What are you doing? Where am I going? What do you want me to do?'

No response.

Nevina was concerned with staying alive. Whilst there was any chance of her calf being born safely, she would hold on. She didn't know how that could happen, but she knew she must hang on. She could breathe, and for the moment that was enough.

She transmitted a familiar sound signature into the water, followed by her own, calling the pod - with a danger signal added. Within minutes they were grouped only fifty metres from her - just outside visual range but in close sonar contact. Heeding the danger signal, and recognising Nevina's plight, they kept their distance. She knew they were there and that gave her comfort.

The hours passed.

Being able to breathe was a mixed blessing. Life continued longer than had been granted to Tanya and Joliba, but in the end that could mean simply enduring the process of death by starvation - not a pleasant prospect.

The other dolphins were powerless to rescue her, but at least they could protect her from predators while she lived.

By now the discarded net had trapped other creatures, including some small squid, and their struggles attracted the sharks. The pod kept watchful eyes on Blue and Mako sharks

9

which appeared looking for an easy meal. One large Blue showed an interest in Nevina until two of the pod rammed him together in his side hard enough to warn him off. It worked - easy meals were not supposed to fight back - and he sped quickly away.

The night came, and passed slowly. The pod kept their vigil. In the new day they went off in turns to feed. Nevina was in pain, not for herself but for her calf and what was in prospect for him. She had resigned herself to her fate, even accepted it. She could simply stop breathing and die if she wished. Yet while her calf lived inside her that was not an option. She had an overpowering compulsion to hold on - for him.

After more than a day in the net the first contraction came. Her body told her that the birth process had started. She fought it. Instead of relaxing and allowing it to happen as she might have done in the freedom of open water, she tensed against it. She would rather they died together than have him emerge from her into that net!

Hold on! Hold on!

For her calf, his experience of the womb had changed totally from life supporting to life threatening. Nevina's tension held him like a vice and now with each contraction, albeit with long intervals between them, he felt crushed beyond endurance. All he knew was that he must get out, and couldn't. However he moved, flexed his body against the pressure, he could find no exit, nowhere to go.

The sun went down on the second day of Nevina's fight for survival. Her tremendous commitment to hold on, to tense against the birth process had prolonged it, but it was taking its toll. She had not eaten since swimming into the net and she felt herself weakening.

The hours of darkness brought out the nocturnal feeders

10

from their hiding places. Beneath Nevina and the pod some of those hiding places were man made. As the net with its living cargo had drifted in the upper currents, its movement had taken it over the wreck of a ship on the sea bed. Such an addition provided an attractive home for marine life of all kinds and a source of interest for human visitors.

THREE

A small inflatable boat with a rigid hull sped over the dark waters.

There was just enough moonlight for the wet-suited diver controlling the powerful outboard motor to be confident at speed. Like his two similarly clad companions he was excited at the prospect of a night dive on the uncharted wreck they had located some days before. This was the first night since their find that conditions were good enough to allow their adventure.

They were quite a distance from the remote shore where they had launched their boat. Arm muscles ached from hanging on to the ropes along the side tubes for so long.

'How much further Tony?' James shouted from his position on the starboard tube.

'Almost there!' from the steersman. Tony peered intently at the shore, looking for the shadowy landmark he had noted previously opposite the position of the wreck.

Terry, on the port tube, was tense and looking directly ahead. He relished the challenge and adrenalin surge of a dive into the blackness of the sea at night. He was a confident, experienced diver in control of himself and his destiny when beneath the surface. However, in this boat, racing over the waves, someone else in the stern in charge of their direction and speed - he felt out of control, and he did not like it. He had appointed himself lookout from the start, and continued to try and pierce the semi-gloom the boat was penetrating.

Tony throttled back and the boat settled in a different attitude in the water.

'We're really close now,' said Tony, 'I'll take a couple of bearings.'

The engine died.

'Oh damn! It does that sometimes if I throttle back too quickly.'

'That's O.K. It can stay that way while you check our position' said James, enjoying the sudden relief from engine noise.

'Hold the torch will you?'

Tony checked his compass and stared toward features on the shore just visible in the moonlight.

'What was that?!' Terry exclaimed.

'What was what?'

'I don't know. I heard something from over there.' Terry pointed out over the port bow of the boat.

'Be quiet for a moment. Listen.'

Nothing. Then the unmistakeable out-breath, and another.

'Hey! We're diving with dolphins tonight!' James was ecstatic.

'Great, we've got to go in their direction anyway - they're right over the wreck,' said Tony, and re-started the engine.

The boat crept gently forward.

At intervals the explosive exhalations could now be heard clearly, but came no closer. The dolphins were keeping their distance, all except one. A much weaker blow and slower intake of breath were coming from one particular spot in the water. Tony steered toward the sound.

Terry and James had their divers' torches out scanning a tight arc in front of the boat.

Nevina's head and dorsal fin, draped in the monofilament net, broke the surface.

'Oh my God! The poor thing's trapped in one of those damn drift nets.'

Tony took charge.

'O.K. I'll handle the boat. Terry, why don't you take both

torches and keep them on the dolphin. James, mask, snorkel and fins, you don't need your tank. Get in there and see if you can free him - or her.'

All three men carried sharp knives, sheathed and strapped to their legs, as standard equipment when diving.

Terry showed his concern as James slipped into the water. 'Be careful. Don't get caught up yourself.'

Finning very slowly over the last few metres to the entangled dolphin, James could see the net dropping away obliquely into the blackness beyond the torchlight. Getting close enough for eye contact, he could see Nevina's left eye almost closed and he sensed they had arrived just in time. Taking great care he unsheathed his knife and started to cut through sections of the fine netting.

To James's enormous relief, Nevina kept very still, floating patiently at the surface. He had half expected panic and struggle, but he sensed that she understood his purpose. He breathed easily through his snorkel tube, occasionally resting and telling the others of his progress.

Terry offered to take over, but they decided to let James continue. There was no adverse reaction to him, so why change a winning game? More and more of Nevina's body was released until, at last, only her head was still enveloped.

James put away his knife and, gripping the remaining net on either side of the dolphin's head, pulled it toward him. It peeled away from her blowhole, over the melon - the forehead sloping down to her upper jaw - and at last released her beak.

At first she didn't move. Then she opened and closed her jaws two or three times, something she hadn't been able to do since she swam into the net. She took a breath, and James stroked her side, delighting in the smooth touch of her and the absence of the fine netting which had so nearly killed

14

her. Then she swam slowly off out of the torchlight and disappeared toward her waiting companions.

The divers celebrated.

'Brilliant! She's free!'

'I feel marvellous! Well done Jim!'

'I always knew I'd find a use for that knife someday!'

Feeling really pleased with themselves, the question of the wreck came up.

'Are you kidding?! It was worth coming all this way just to free that dolphin!'

'To hell with the dive - nothing we find down there is going to compare with what we've been doing!'

'I'm exhausted now anyway!'

They turned back toward the shore and the distant beach of their launching unaware that they had saved not one life, but two.

FOUR

The pod closed around Nevina, buzzing her with their sonar, welcoming her back to the fold. After the loss of Tanya and Joliba, it was as if Nevina had come back from the dead. She could only move slowly and the others stayed in close support as they made for familiar waters.

She drew on the collective energy of the pod. With that and the freshly caught fish her companions provided for her, she gained in strength.

The dawn of a new day threw light into the surface which reflected off the backs of the six dolphins moving steadily through the water.

Nevina's initial fear at the appearance of the divers had changed to confusion. Their intentions were clearly benevolent, and their actions had saved her and her unborn calf. Yet the net was a human creation designed to catch and kill marine life at random. These extremes of her encounters with humans baffled her.

Nevina's close contact with the diver in the water had given her strong images and feelings around this alien presence in her environment. Her confusion had given way to intense curiosity. Weak as she had been she hadn't been able to resist checking him with her sonar when he was in front of her removing the net from her head.

All of which had an impact on her calf. He was imprinted with images of the human shape and many different thoughts and feelings attaching to it as Nevina went through her part of this human/dolphin interaction. His life would continue because of that interaction and be influenced profoundly by it.

Throughout her rescue Nevina had not had a contraction,

but now the birth process re-asserted itself.

The pod was on the fringes of its normal feeding grounds when her body contracted sharply. Traumatised though she had been, now, at last, she could let go and surrender to what was about to happen.

'It's alright little one, now we can be two.' Nevina sent the thought to her calf within.

Her calf was only dimly aware of her assurance - he was too busy surviving the sudden increase in pressure on every part of his body. His overwhelming drive was to escape, to get out of this place where it felt to him as if his very survival was now at risk. He felt crushed.

Nevina's body took over and she rejoiced that she no longer had to fight or obstruct the birth. The contractions came on rapidly.

Sometimes a spurt of fear prompted a brief return of the tension, the holding on. Then a deeper knowing, a trust in the process took over and she let go again. The peaks of pain were new to her and tolerable only because she knew they must come to an end soon. As Nevina let go more and more she responded to her calf's distress with powerful thoughts.

'We're starting a new life. You are to live in a larger world. This is normal, natural. You are safe. We will be together for as long as you want.'

She held a picture in her mind of her calf, relaxed, surrendered, giving up to a process over which he had no conscious control.

This time more of her desire to communicate got through. He felt her response to him, felt something of her love and reassurance. He let go his desire to fight for survival. The inevitability of the birth process overcame him again and again, and the more he surrendered to it, the less threatening the pressure of his mother's contractions became.

Nevina's back arched and his small, perfectly formed tail flukes emerged from her. She gave a few vigorous strokes of her own tail. The undulating movement felt good and she knew it was time for him to leave her body. The most powerful reaction she had ever known arose in her body and she arched her back again in response to it. At last, as she straightened finally, he was free and swimming energetically, bounding to the surface for his first independent breath.

With a sense of wonder at the creative act she had been involved in, and not a little relief that her new calf looked strong and healthy, Nevina moved alongside him. They would be swimming closely together, matching each other's movements, for some months yet. Then he would start to venture away from her side until, by the time he was two years old, just the occasional sonar contact would be enough. By then he would be feeding and fending for himself.

Having explored him with the higher frequencies of her sonar, reassuring herself that everything internally was as it should be, Nevina received a name for him, as she knew she would.

Boji, the bringer of balance.

At once she rejoiced in it and wondered what life would bring him with a name like that. At the same time she noticed a blue tinge to the normal grey of his skin. It was particularly evident where the darker, upper body colour changed to the white of the underbelly. She warmed to that distinctive tinge. She knew he could have been any colour of the multi-hued reef fish she played with occasionally, and she would still love it as part of her unconditional love for her first-born.

There appeared a brief knot of fear within her as she wondered how that difference would be received by others in the pod.

Boji was unaware of both his colouring and his mother's reactions. Now he was swimming freely in the sunlit water new feelings and sensations assailed him - and he loved it.

Other members of the pod came in close and bombarded him with love and messages of welcome.

His mother never left his side and he enjoyed following her every movement, falling easily into her breathing rhythms. He felt the security of her presence, sensing and receiving the continual body contact between them. Thoughts, images, feelings pulsed back and forth. Nevina would celebrate the sheer joy of her new motherhood with a barrel roll or a somersault, with Boji alongside wondering what was going on as he slid down his mother's flank.

FIVE

Boji learned fast in the days and weeks that followed.

He got used to conscious breathing, the need for fresh air prompting the thought, the thought prompting the action, perfecting the quick loop toward the bright, reflective roof of his world.

Energy he had in plenty, resting only an occasional need. He followed his mother's patterns of periods of stillness spent just below the surface in a state of deep relaxation, rising gently with her when a breath became necessary.

Feeding was easy and fun. Nudging at Nevina's belly he rolled his tongue into a watertight tube and received jet after jet of rich warm milk as she squeezed it from her body. He didn't even have to suck.

Two or three times a day the dolphins of home pod would feed, and though he took no active part he enjoyed swimming fast with his mother through a shoal of fish surrounded by the pod whilst she took what she needed.

Once, he was separated briefly from her to find himself face to face with a barracuda surveying the tasty shoal from a distance. The fish was about as long as he was and built for speed. He felt some fear, but curiosity kept him in place until Nevina found him and steered him away.

'We are not the only ones to take fish from the larger shoals Boji. There are many like that one. Whilst there is plenty for all we are not enemies.'

And plenty there seemed to be.

Sometimes the pod would break up and feed singly. It was then that Boji was most aware of a language as yet unknown to him. He could feel strange noises in his head - clicks, squeals, buzzes and deeper vibrations. He accepted them as part of the constant background sound of the ocean, but at times they became intrusive and demanding, especially when his mother was feeding on her own. He felt some of them were aimed at him and realised he was supposed to be trying to copy them. He had no idea yet how to do that and Nevina seemed happy that he had noticed the difference from the other ways she had of communicating with him. She would dart off at high speed and the intensity of sound would build quickly to a peak which he felt rather than heard, then she would appear with a large juicy fish in her mouth, letting him see it before swallowing it.

Boji's home pod was a small one, apart from his mother there were three other adult females and two of their offspring, males still young enough to want to stay in the same pod as their mothers for the time being. Visits were frequent, and interactions with other pods a joy.

One such visit turned out to be rather special. Boji's sensitivity told him his mother and his 'aunties' in the pod were excited and communicating more than usual. Long range messages were being beamed out and answered from a distant pod.

'What's going on?' Boji moved in tight to his mother's side, but had to work hard to stay with her.

'You'll see Boji', and she leapt clear of the water, re-entering with hardly a ripple.

He enjoyed the games, Nevina had not been as playful as this since he had been born. He knew her love and gentleness, this was a part of her that was new to him.

She rejoiced in her body, moving fast through the water, rolling, swimming inverted, leaping, and breaching - letting herself smash back into the water on her side, creating an enormous splash after hurling herself into the air.

Boji couldn't keep up with all of it but he did his best,

blowing frequently, often by his own choice when he felt the need.

The connecting pod arrived and the energy was quite different. Fully grown male dolphins of all ages were suddenly joining in the games.

Boji swam in close to his mother's body, unsure of this new situation yet excited and full of an energy he hadn't felt before.

The adults were pairing off and powering through the water together, blowing, leaping and breaching in unison.

The largest dolphin Boji had yet seen moved in close to the other side of Nevina. For the first time since his birth her attention was centred on someone other than Boji. Even before she sent him the message to confirm it, Boji was aware this newcomer was his father. Close to a metre longer than Nevina, he was heavier in the body and his colouring was much darker. The differences in body shape were very subtle but obvious to Boji. His father's tail stock was deeper, his dorsal fin longer with a trailing edge that looked ragged compared with the clean lines of Nevina's.

The water was full of noise, everyone was communicating at once, high pitched buzzes and clicks assailed Boji's senses. His father's presence dominated his feelings but Boji felt no fear, he was bathed in love of a different quality from that of his mother.

Briefly, he was the focus of attention from both his parents.

'Yes Boji, this is your father Ananda. I see much of him in you. Know him, be with him while you can.'

Boji glowed with delight, somersaulting twice beneath them for sheer joy.

Then suddenly they existed solely for each other and Boji could only watch and wonder. They undulated gently

22

through the water, bodies sliding against each other. His father nipped Nevina's tail flukes and dorsal with his powerful jaws. She responded by opening her mouth wide and flicking her head sideways against him, her teeth leaving rake marks on his skin, and then dashing away at full speed, to be caught again in moments.

Boji had never seen Nevina do anything so violent, yet all the feelings and vibrations he was getting from them were high levels of excitement and pleasure.

Nevina threw herself at the surface and levelled off, swimming fast, her dorsal fin cleaving through the water. Ananda followed, and after blowing twice very quickly, chased after her to swim inverted beneath her, moving in close in perfect unison.

Boji felt the ecstatic explosion of their joining. He had no idea how that had been achieved, but he didn't care. He had felt at second hand something of the beauty, the love and the playfulness of it all, and that was enough. There was a special joy in feeling the oneness of these two most important beings in his life.

SIX

Ananda and his pod stayed for a while, and each day was spent in playing, feeding and lovemaking. The next generation of dolphins for Nevina's pod were conceived in an aura of celebration of their time together.

Boji enjoyed this new dimension to his life. He was over half the length of his mother now, and growing fast. Venturing away from Nevina's side became more and more attractive, particularly whilst his father was around. The games Ananda played were different, more challenging to Boji's increasing awareness of his abilities, physically stretching him.

Ananda came close one morning after feeding well on the high tide, trying to squeeze between Boji and his mother. The two of them spent a few playful, delicious moments pretending they didn't want that to happen, twisting and turning to keep Boji away from Ananda's lunges. Giving up keeping him at bay, Boji peeled away from Nevina and joined his father.

'Come Boji, today we learn something new, the sea is right for it.'

Ananda increased speed and headed toward the distant shore.

Moving easily up to fifteen knots Boji found he could keep pace. Clearly his father had power to spare but seemed to know what Boji's limits were and kept to them.

With each breath it was obvious that the mood of the sea was violent. The heavy swell changed from rounded mountains and valleys to sharper, steeper waves as they approached the shore.

'Stay close Boji, and do as I do.'

Ananda hung in the water, just beneath the surface, and

Boji did as he was told. It seemed far too near to the land, but he trusted his father and waited for his next move.

The surge of a mighty wave lifted them both and Ananda let loose clicks of delight and swam with the wave toward the shore. Boji followed feeling very unsure of himself. The bulk of the wave was changing shape, growing in height, creating a long ridge of water. As it peaked and started to roll over, Ananda turned sharply and threw himself high into the wave. Swimming very fast parallel to the shore, he kept just ahead of the breaking edge of the wave as it rolled over and crashed down into the shallows.

Boji stayed with him, just, and in the midst of the buffeting he was getting he wondered if he was supposed to be enjoying this!

As the wave lost its power, Ananda leapt out of the rounded seaward side of it and dashed several hundred metres out to sea again.

When Boji joined him, Ananda was really energised.

'One more, then you can lead. Wait...wait...this one, let's go!'

They were off in another huge wave. This time his father went further ahead of the breaking point of the wave, giving Boji a smoother ride close behind.

He began to feel differently about it. It was like flying through the air on a very long, fast leap, but he was still in a supporting tower of water - wow!

Now it was his turn to lead. With mounting impatience he waited for the right wave, but it was worth it. A mass of water rushed in on them, larger than the others, and Boji was off, Ananda right on his tail. The moment of turning along the wave was critical and Boji almost waited too long, but his father urged him on.

'Now Boji, now!'

They turned and Boji was swimming faster than he had ever done - he was flying - helped on by the energy of the wave.

'Out!' from his father, and they leapt out of the back of the wave just as it finally sacrificed itself to the rocks reaching up to claim its energy.

'You've got it Boji!'

They leapt and breached in delight as they raced back to deeper water together.

Boji spent many happy hours with his father, and the joy he found in learning knew no bounds.

He had started experimenting with his sonar some time before and his mother had helped him to the basics through patient repetition of certain sounds. Once Boji had got the idea that he had to retain air and use it to create a sound inside him and not blast it out of his blowhole, Nevina had a job to stop him making all sorts of weird, indecipherable noises. He worked on refining the movement of air through the tiny passages and membranes in his head until he was producing a range of sounds almost as broad as his mother's. He adopted a sound 'signature' resembling that of Nevina but different enough to make it unique to him. With practice, he learnt about the quality of the returning echoes and what they meant - particularly what was good to eat and what was not. Some of the frequencies he was using passed right through flesh, reflecting back only from the bone and air spaces within the body of the creatures he scanned. When he first discovered that facility he used it on his parents continually until he knew them inside and out - literally.

Ananda helped him to learn how to focus and direct the sounds he made. Boji was astonished how much he could learn about his surroundings from the returning echoes. He could keep track of the rest of the pod, where they were and what they were doing. He could locate prey within easy distance, and place himself relative to the surface, the sea bed, rocks, wrecks, reefs, and any other feature of his environment. All of this at the same time, if he chose, and without seeing any of them.

Ananda demonstrated the deeper frequencies and just how far they could carry through the water. They were sounds that Boji felt rather than heard. All the returning echoes were like that but the power and depth of sound his father used to connect with other dolphins over great distances really set Boji vibrating. He tried to copy what Ananda was doing but as yet the range was not available to him.

'It will come in time Boji.' His father reassured him.

The months passed and, whilst Boji spent much of his time alongside his mother, he looked forward increasingly to Ananda's visits and the expanding horizons they presented. He was eager to learn how to feed himself and Ananda showed him the best fish to go for and those to avoid.

At around two metres long Boji was a little over two thirds the size of his mother, and still reliant on her milk or fish that she caught for him. He tried repeatedly to produce that build up of high frequency sound which both his parents and the other adult dolphins employed so successfully when feeding. Many times he would echolocate a healthy fish of the right size, give chase, and getting close enough to his prey, build up to the loudest sound he could, only to see his prospective meal dart away unharmed.

Ananda helped him solve the problem eventually by transmitting to him two acoustic images - one large and diffuse, like Boji's attempts, and the other small and very concentrated, as it needed to be.

With that in his mind Boji's efforts started yielding some success. At last his prey were disoriented enough for him to grab them. Nothing before or after was to taste quite so delicious as the very first fish he caught unaided.

SEVEN

As Boji approached the end of his first year Nevina fed him less and less. Partly from habit, and partly because he still wanted the closeness and feelings of security it gave him, he still nudged his mother's underbelly for milk. She gradually reduced the proportion of supply to his demand and then stopped feeding him altogether when it was clear he had mastered the art of feeding himself. By then he was fourteen months old and still the seventh and youngest member of the pod. Not for much longer however. Two of the adult females were heavily pregnant from that first wonderful visit Boji had witnessed from Ananda and his companions. Home pod would soon be nine. Boji's attachment to it was still strong but more elastic. He joined in communal feeding when a shoal was surrounded and individual fish in it were taken at leisure. He swam alongside Nevina occasionally. However, increasingly he enjoyed going off on his own and inventing solitary games and activities.

One particular pleasure he had discovered on one of Ananda's visits, which were becoming much less frequent. They had swum together away from the coast and the shallow water which was all Boji had known until then. The sea bed had been no more than fifty to a hundred metres beneath him, and swimming over water of six or seven times that depth both excited and frightened him at first.

Eventually Ananda slowed to a halt.

'Today we'll dive together, and you will learn more of how your body works.'

They hung at the surface for a moment.

'Follow me and trust!'

Boji did as he was told. They took three breaths in quick succession and angled gently downward. Approaching a depth of one hundred metres, Boji had the sensation in his chest which he recognised from playing near the sea bed closer inshore. A feeling of contraction, no pain but he felt threatened by it and started to level out.

The messages from Ananda were powerful as he continued down.

'No, keep going Boji. You're quite safe. Let it happen. Watch my chest, it's quite normal.'

Boji noticed that the outline of his father's body was changing, becoming slimmer behind his fins. He forced his head down again and accelerated. He hadn't been this far from the surface before and he was uncomfortably aware that the life-giving air was getting further and further away. Still no pain, but it felt very strange to have his ribs collapsing inward, and he hoped this was what his father meant by 'normal'.

They reached two hundred metres. Ananda levelled out.

'You see Boji, all is well. We could go a lot deeper, our bodies can take it. When you get used to the changes it can be fun!'

Boji wished he felt as confident as his father, but he had to admit this was something special. It promised many new challenges, adventures, discoveries. The attraction of delving deeply into himself and his environment had started to exert its fascination. For the moment, he was relieved when Ananda beamed at him.

'Race you to the surface!'

No more than five minutes had elapsed since their last in-breath. Boji was still glad to see the sunshine penetrating the upper layers of water, and finally to break into the air with an explosion of out-breath a split second after his father.

EIGHT

After his dive with Ananda Boji found that he was drawn to the deeper water. Somehow he knew that he could learn much more and much faster by moving away from home pod's usual haunts along the coast.

As he advanced well into his second year and felt his burgeoning power and endurance he longed to test himself, push against his limits, or at least those he had known until then.

Many times he would drop below the rest of the pod in mid-water, and follow the sea bed, swimming away from the coastline. Nevina would call him, sending out her own sound signature followed by Boji's. He would respond, repeating his own distinct set of sounds to reassure her, then turning back as he sensed the growing urgency and concern in her distant calls. Although Boji always seemed to return unharmed, his mother's anxiety for his safety increased as he went further and deeper into the ocean.

He was pleased with himself when he surpassed the two hundred metres he had reached with his father.

The waters frequented by home pod were ideal for his learning. The sea bed shelved gently away so his progress was easy to control and monitor. When he had gone as far as he could he turned smoothly up into the vertical and made for the light and air far above him. There came a time when he reached a level of performance he could not improve upon by this method, a faster, more direct descent was needed. Even so he had reached more than twice the depth of that original dive with Ananda, and had gained greater confidence in his body and its abilities.

One bright, cool morning in his second Autumn found

him in his favourite situation - alone over deep water. Curving easily to the surface he pushed the used air in his lungs up and out through his blowhole in an explosive out-breath, and refilled with fresh air, all in half a second. In quick succession he repeated the operation two, three times more and then dived straight down.

The light from the surface faded into deep blue and then black as he covered the first hundred metres in a few seconds. He used his sonar in every direction and the returning echoes told him the sea was clear of obstruction for miles around - no rock formations, no ships on the surface or wrecks beneath it. The only substantial echo came from the sea bed so he knew how much space he had beneath him.

Boji was excited, for he knew if he could reach five hundred metres this morning it would be his deepest dive yet. At two hundred metres he became aware of his body adjusting to the water pressure. He was familiar now with the feeling of his chest caving inwards and the air compressing and moving into his windpipe and nasal sacs and passages. There was no pain, just a sense of gratitude that he had a body capable of handling deep dives.

Three hundred metres passed. Around three hundred and fifty metres he slowed. His blood circulation was concentrated around the vital organs. With less available to his extremities, he was dependent on the oxygen stored in the muscle tissue to keep him moving.

He started to level out. He hadn't gone beyond four hundred and fifty metres along the sea bed. His way ahead was still clear, the last shoal of fish was now above him as he broadcast on two frequencies, one narrow band and one broad band - the echoes reassured him.

Four hundred metres and he could feel his heart labouring. The need to take another breath was asserting itself. He forced his body downward, the blackness beckoned. Again at four hundred and fifty metres he knew he could go no further. He turned for the surface, his hopes dashed.

Already looking forward to his next attempt he consoled himself with thoughts of his comparative youth, and yet he knew there was much more to his search than just finding his physical limitations.

There was the mystery, so many questions without answers. Even the questions were, as yet, largely unformed in him. The drive to learn was powerful. Boji's greatest pleasures were to be found in the expansion necessary to seek out and convert the unfamiliar to the familiar, the unknown to the known.

Nevina never tried to stop his expeditions, but she let him know that she would have preferred him to spend more time in and around the pod, sharing in what she regarded as normal activities -playing and releasing his excess energy with the other young male dolphins in the pod.

In fact, on many occasions he had attempted to do just that, and had encountered a lot of rejection and ridicule as a result.

Boji's mother was not the only member of home pod to have feelings about his delight in solitary pursuits. Now that he was approaching full size and strength, his presence in support of the rest of the pod was expected as a matter of course. For the others, his absence was seen to be critical following a close encounter with predators which could have resulted in the destruction of the pod.

NINE

Boji had fed well with the rest of the pod on a late morning high tide. As their hunger was sated and a calmer energy took over, he slipped away into deeper water anticipating more lone adventures. He travelled further than usual, moving directly away from the coast.

Fruitlessly attempting to maintain sonar contact with him, Nevina had pulled the pod with her a considerable distance into the open ocean. However, there came a time when her urgings had taken them as far as they were prepared to go for this errant son of hers. They turned back as one for the shore, pushing out sonar signals ahead seeking familiar echoes to guide them. Instead they detected a strange scene which had appeared between themselves and home waters.

A small ship was cruising across their path and, though rare in this part of the sea, that in itself was not perceived as a threat.

What was unusual was what was happening behind the craft in the water. It was trailing long lines with clusters of metal objects attached at regular intervals, and beneath these were thirty to forty sharks.

The dolphins instinctively slowed and drew closer together. On an equal footing they knew they could deal with sharks if necessary, but in this situation they were heavily outnumbered and if the sharks were hungry they could be in danger.

What was the attraction? Why so many sharks?

Then all became clear. Something fell into the water immediately behind the ship, the sharks fled in all directions, there was a sharp explosion, and they returned to feed on a few dead and stunned fish in the wake. Not enough to satisfy their voracious appetites, for some of them had seen the eight dolphins, almost stationary, and glided back to investigate. Very soon the attractions of a vulnerable pod of dolphins, particularly one which included two very young calves, had pulled most of the sharks away from the back of the ship.

Nevina, the other three adult females, and the two young males formed a tight circle around the calves and picked up speed for home territory.

The sharks had the pod outnumbered by at least four to one and their confidence increased. The prospect of young dolphin meat excited them. They circled the dolphins, gradually swimming faster and getting closer.

Nevina started sending loud communicating noises into the water, and the others followed suit, in the hope of confusing the hungry predators. That only seemed to make things worse. The sharks became more agitated in their movements and one, bolder than the rest, made a fast run at the pod. The bigger of the two young males lunged at it and missed as it turned away at high speed.

A second shark made for them. This time the same young dolphin managed to turn and butt the attacker hard in its side.

Temporarily the shark lost balance in the water and swam awkwardly away. Such vulnerability was enough. The creature was immediately set upon by its own kind and torn to pieces.

The feeding frenzy was a distraction and home pod moved on their way as fast as the young calves could manage. Not for long. The larger, faster sharks soon caught up with them, forcing Nevina and the others to slow again within a lethal ring of sleek, ruthless bodies with razor sharp teeth.

The former pattern resumed, and, coming to a halt, the six dolphins turned outwards to face their fate, with the two young calves in the centre frightened and confused.

The challenging runs started again, this time in twos and threes. The dolphins waited for an opportunity to strike a telling blow without venturing too far from the pod. Much depended on the next few moments.

Then, without warning, the energy surrounding them changed.

The dolphins' sonar detected a number of large body masses approaching the outer circle of sharks, which started to break up.

Huge black and white bodies moved with amazing speed and agility amongst the sharks, who were now concerned with their own survival much more than a meal of dolphin.

Nevina identified the newcomers in sight and sound - Orca! The whale called Killer!

A large bull Orca, at least eight metres long, drifted across her vision. He was toying with a shark in his jaws as easily as a dolphin might play with a salmon. She realised their earlier frantic transmissions of sound had probably attracted the Orcas.

With powerful thoughts and body contact Nevina urged the others into movement. It was one thing to be faced with hungry sharks and have a chance of driving them off. Against Orcas there was no defence - and she knew it. A transient pod of Orcas looking for food would take anything that crossed its path, including other whales and dolphins.

The adults in the pod knew their only hope was to go for shallow water as fast as they could and hope that the Orcas' meal of sharks would satisfy them. The dolphins sped homeward, leaving behind the carnage in the water. If they felt the Orcas' sonar reaching for them that would be the end.

Minutes went by and no vibrations touched them.

Eventually the familiar coastline appeared and the sea bottom shelved up towards them. Slowing to a halt, they stayed silent, knowing that if they sent sonar searching back the way they had come, that might only serve to attract the Orcas again.

Hours passed with no sign of the ocean's number one predators.

Gradually they relaxed, rejoicing in their survival and in the bonding their experiences that day had served to strengthen even further.

That bonding did not include Boji.

He hadn't been with them when the very life of the pod had been threatened. Worse than that, his wanderings that day were seen as the cause of the whole incident. He became the subject of clear messages of disapproval from his peers. When he did try to join their games they either swam off or ganged up on him. He had many more rake marks and scars from their teeth than a dolphin of his age would have normally.

Even the adults in the pod had started to avoid him.

He was hurt and confused in his increasing isolation.

'What's wrong with me?' he asked his mother. 'I don't understand why they do what they do.'

'You grow strong Boji,' she answered, 'but you are still young, and your home is where we are. Some are even saying none of it would have happened if you had been with us instead of off on your own. Can you not be with us more my son? We are coastal dolphins, we spend our time together in shallow waters where the fish are plentiful. Our survival depends on our support for one another. It's not natural for you to spend so much time alone, far away in the open ocean.'

Boji's deep love for Nevina prompted a change. For a while he did his best to comply with his mother's wishes. He stayed close to shore and fed with the pod. He was still shunned by the other young dolphins, but he ignored the barbs and the jeers.

He went through the motions, but felt increasingly frustrated. It isn't working, he thought, avoiding an aggressive lunge by one of the other young males who did not like having Boji around.

Very soon he went back to playing the games he much preferred - those he invented and played on his own.

He loved competing with himself, leaping higher and higher out of the water and measuring the highest point he could reach by a familiar rock jutting steeply out of the sea.

Boji spent whole days alone, sometimes even forgetting to take time out to feed himself. His fascination with testing himself to the limit made his isolation almost complete, but that bothered him less and less. What he was doing was far more exciting to him than the games the other young dolphins were playing.

In shallow water with the sun high he began making fast runs over recognisable sections of the sea bed only ten metres beneath him. Always leaping at full speed from a point over one particular kelp bed, when he re-entered the water he turned round immediately and noted where the shadow of the splash fell on the sand of the sea floor. He was happy learning the optimum speed, best trajectory, the timing of the last thrust of his tail before leaving the water, everything that would make his leaps longer and longer.

His experiments diving in deep water took up more of his time and energy. He felt at home, far out to sea, over water a thousand metres deep, doing what he enjoyed most, pushing at his limits, challenging himself.

TEN

As is the case with all dolphins, each breath Boji took was the result of a conscious decision. Breathing and the effects of varying it held his interest. He had noticed that others of his pod took only what they needed to support them in what they were doing - resting, feeding, playing, travelling. Their efficiency in making use of the air in their lungs was taken for granted.

For Boji this was another area of discovery and he was learning how to make a joyous, creative act of every breath. He lived to breathe and dive, whilst others breathed to live.

He also tried different techniques of descent while repeating a similar breathing pattern before each deep diving attempt. He spent weeks comparing the merits of relaxing and letting himself fall into the depths - at most using a gentle undulation of his body as the only propulsion - as against swimming powerfully downward as fast as he could. One method conserved oxygen but took longer, the other used up his air reserves quickly, but gave him a fast descent.

Diving again over a deep trench he had found in the sea bed, Boji pushed the air out of his lungs and refilled six times in quick succession before rolling over and dropping steeply, slowly downward. He resisted the urge to use the tremendous boost of energy such breathing gave him and relaxed into an easy rhythm of movement curving toward the trench beneath him.

After a minute or so he was over three hundred metres down, feeling good, still relaxed, if a little impatient with his progress. Dropping easily into the darkness anxiety gnawed at him. Five, or even ten minutes beneath the surface in shallow water was not a problem, but that time limit changed drastically as depth increased. The shoulder of the trench appeared and slipped past, registering on the broad band sonar he was transmitting.

At four hundred metres the desire to tense all the muscles of his body and force himself through the water faster was overwhelming. Instead, he flattened his pectoral fins along his body and tried instructing himself repeatedly to let go and relax.

He opened his eyes, peering down in the hope of seeing the deep swimming creatures, fish and crustaceans which provided their own sources of light from within their bodies. Such distractions were not presenting themselves this time.

Near his limit he was still winning the battle to stay relaxed - just! His body and the survival patterns in his mind were shouting at him to race for the surface. No, you're alright, let go, let go, he thought, it's working! He started hallucinating, seeing his mother swimming close alongside him as she had done when he was a small calf.

Dimly, he knew he had broken through to five hundred metres but had no time to rejoice. He turned upward and the survival energy took over. He bulleted for the surface. Even as he was losing his grip on consciousness his body beat the water. Thirty seconds later in a daze of pain, and no longer caring what happened, he hit the surface. Gasping out the stale air, he lolled helpless for several minutes, recovering, grateful for the gift of the salt air searing into his oxygen starved body.

He felt he should be pleased with himself - a new frontier, a new depth record for him of five hundred metres but his only sense was one of failure, there was so much more to explore. The sea bed for so much of the ocean was still far beneath his measly five hundred metres - and that had nearly killed him! The weight of failure was heavy on his back, and the thought crossed his mind how good it would be to go down and never come up again.

A voice of resignation pressed him from within. This is crazy. I am a dolphin with a body which has its limits, and I'm not meant to go beyond them. If I were meant to learn so much about breathing and diving deeply and staying at depth for long periods, I'd be one of the big baleen whales, like a Blue or a Fin; or one of the larger toothed whales like the Sperm Whale. Mother was right. I must put all this behind me. I must return to the home pod and be what I am - a limited coastal dolphin.

Boji found himself agreeing with the voice. He would be close to shore and take his place with the others, be a normal dolphin. Perhaps then members of the pod would accept him, and Nevina would be happier.

He turned away from the deep water and swam slowly toward the land, glad that he had learned something about himself and economy of movement. No! Enough, he thought, that is past history. I am finished with learning. I have everything I need to survive - what more do I want. I am a dolphin like any other dolphin, and I will live like one.

With that he picked up speed and pushed on for the shore, some of his muscles still protesting from their bout of oxygen starvation.

He felt a sense of relief now that he had decided to be just another one of the pod. That compulsive attachment to learning had gone. Never mind what was waiting for him in the depths, it could wait! No more feelings of inadequacy and failure. It was easy, just stop searching and swim through the darkness toward the echoes returning to him from the distant shore. The night served to emphasize his sense of aloneness.

The voice welled up again. You should be with the

others, resting quietly, close to shore, just beneath the surface, bobbing gently up to breathe when the need arises. What are you doing?!

Boji didn't listen. He didn't need the light to move around safely. In any case, it's beautiful, he thought. The surface of the sea so black, reflecting the moon and stars.

He turned over and swam inverted for a while, watching the brightness of tiny phosphorescent creatures flare briefly in his wake.

He berated himself gently as he moved through the water. For once, the permanent smile built into the curve of his jaws, hid genuine amusement. You must have been mad! You could have killed yourself you idiot! Going off alone, diving that deep. Supposing something had gone seriously wrong, there was no one to help you. The voice reminded him. If you were meant to dive so deeply and spend so long down there, you would have the lungs and the huge body of a Blue Whale! You would breathe like a Sperm Whale!

He stopped dead in the water. Boji the Blue Dolphin hung vertically, squeezed his eyes shut and blasted a gout of air out of his blowhole. The big bubbles mushroomed up to the surface. His pain and his decision to conform disappeared. A Sperm Whale. Breathe like a Sperm Whale! That's it! I've been so impatient to dive I've only ever taken a few breaths, and always the same kind of breath, before going under. I'm not giving myself a chance.

Memories came flooding in of his one and only encounter with a group of Great Sperm Whales far out to sea. The returning echoes of his sonar bouncing back from their bone structure and air spaces within their bodies had told him of their enormous size. As he had approached them, warily at first, his curiosity greater than his fear, they had shown not the slightest interest in him, continuing their leisurely pace through the water.

There were nine of them, including two young calves twice his size, very close together, bodies rubbing against each other as they swam. He had sensed their peaceful, pleasurable mood, and gaining in confidence, moved in to get a good look. Boji remembered how he had been in awe of them and had noticed their breathing pattern before a dive.

He had watched an adult male, some sixteen metres long, spend about ten minutes at the surface breathing deeply every ten seconds or so. He must have taken at least fifty breaths, then his great head went down, his tail flukes came up out of the water, and he had disappeared almost vertically into the depths.

Boji had remained where he was to see how long the whale stayed down. As the minutes went by he remembered wondering if something had happened, he couldn't believe that it was possible for any living thing dependent on air to live could stay without it for so long.

Eventually, about forty five minutes later, the Sperm Whale had surfaced right alongside the rest of his group and his first exhalation was like an explosion.

That wasn't the kind of meeting Boji was likely to forget.

He recalled it now as he turned and accelerated back toward the deep trench full of excitement and expectation.

Locating the deep water beneath him again, he started to breathe like the Sperm Whale he had watched during that wonderful encounter. Breathing out slowly, taking about three seconds for the exhalation, Boji gave himself a second for each intake of air. It felt strange at first, he was used to emptying and refilling his lungs much faster, but he persevered. After about twenty breaths he found himself getting impatient to dive, but he made himself stay at the surface and count the breaths. He felt increasingly powerful, his body was singing with energy. His fins, tail flukes, and an area around his jaws all started tingling. He kept at it, like the Sperm Whale! At last, after counting fifty breaths, he leapt into the air, tucked his fins in tight to his sides, re-entered the water with hardly a ripple, and sped downward into the blackness beneath him.

Within seconds he was moving at twenty five knots almost straight down. Three hundred metres came and went. Now he accepted his body adjusting to the increasing pressure without a second thought. Four hundred, five hundred metres, and still plenty of energy in reserve. Suddenly, here was the sea bed rushing up to meet him. Six hundred metres! And it was easier than it had been before at five hundred. He flattened out and glided over the sea floor, his presence unseen, but sensed by the myriad creatures of the permanent night of the depths. He celebrated with two fast barrel rolls - six hundred metres, and with time and energy to spare this time.

What a pity I wasn't over a deeper part of the ocean, he thought, if I used that kind of breathing again I wonder how deep......

ELEVEN

At dawn, Boji was practising again. He had swum further away from home pod than ever before, though he maintained a remote connection with the deeper frequencies of his sonar. At that level, the sea carried the sound for many kilometres, and his 'signature' was instantly recognised and returned by the others.

He had never felt so alive. He was experimenting with variations on the theme of how to breathe more and more effectively, changing the times spent on inhaling and exhaling. The results were encouraging.

He had to be careful though. He had been deliberately panting at one stage, and the unusual vibrations had made some sharks very inquisitive. Anything that is out of the ordinary, or might denote vulnerability among the creatures of the sea will suggest the prospect of a meal to a shark. Four or five of them appeared out of the depths and started circling Boji - not a good sign! He immediately took two straightforward dolphin breaths and dived, calling with his sonar to an imaginary pod nearby. He knew he could have dealt with one or two of the sharks, but more than that and he decided his best weapon was to return to normal, healthy dolphin behaviour. It worked. They lost interest very quickly and didn't even follow his dive.

Now, alone again, he had found an area of the deepest water he had yet swum over.

He breathed differently again, conscious of every in-breath and slowing it down, then letting the out-breath take care of itself. He still copied the multiple breaths of the big Sperm Whale and then, tingling with energy again, dropped like a stone. He pushed hard, his body streamlined and perfectly adapted to his environment, creating virtually no drag at all.

Another wonderful by-product to all this was the additional speed he had found. At the surface he could bound along at well over thirty five knots now, and he thought, if I can do that, then why not when I'm diving. Sure enough, that morning he hit thirty five knots straight down and six hundred metres deep with ease.

He kept going, he couldn't believe how good he felt. Eight hundred metres and he knew he was deeper than any dolphin had ever been before.

Other experiences were coming to him at that depth. He knew the sea was much more than he had previously imagined. It was a living entity which supported and loved him, and he could make a conscious choice to play in it, to enjoy it to the full, and to love it as he had felt its love for him.

He somersaulted at speed, ending up not knowing which way was up. Laughing at himself he sent echoes out in all directions to get his bearings. The sea bed was another two hundred metres down but he was content to be where he was, rejoicing in his discoveries, and the freedom he had found.

He knew he had made a breakthrough.

He had never felt so free.

We're not nearly as limited as we think we are, he thought. Our boundaries are much broader and more fluid than we believe.

He could hardly wait to share with the others what he had discovered about the profound effects of breathing, diving and behaving in ways other than the norm. What a difference it could make to everyone, if they would only give it a try!

He arched his back and swam slowly through a long deliberate loop. As he completed it he accelerated, pulling up into a steep climb toward the surface. Exultant, he moved faster and faster. His new found feelings of expansion and personal freedom made it alright, more than that, a delight, a celebration, to be Boji the Blue Dolphin. Self-doubt and condemnation had gone, for the moment at least.

In his excitement he didn't use his sonar as he shot upwards.

The Orcas in his path had positioned themselves carefully to let him through the centre of their pod. They were at the limit of light penetration of the sea, so at the last moment Boji was dimly aware of firing between some very large body masses before reaching the blessed air.

He breathed quickly, ready for instant flight.

Too late.

Two large bull Orcas moved in close.

Boji thought his last moment had come. Neither fight nor flight were possible. He needed time to recover from his great diving adventure of that morning, and they were more than twice his length, and many times his weight and power.

'Have no fear, we are well fed,' came from the senior of the two, 'but you must come with us.'

This is not the time to demonstrate independence, thought Boji. I wonder what they want. They turned for the distant shore.

'Where are you taking me?' asked Boji. There was no reply, except a gentle acceleration. Boji kept station between them and said no more.

Despite his fear of his Orca escorts, he could not help admiring them. It's not often a dolphin gets this close to an Orca without being its next meal, he thought.

Once he got used to their presence as a non-threatening one he realised, with a thrill, he was in yet another learning situation.

Their markings were distinct, black above and white below, with a white patch above and behind the eye, and a white extension curving up and along the side the shape of a long slim fin. Boji noticed the extremes of their colouring - the black was the deepest he had ever seen, and he couldn't imagine anything whiter than the white markings on their bodies.

The sheer size of them, coupled with a feeling of tremendous power and certainty left Boji in no doubt as to why Orcas hold the dominant position in the food chain. He knew nothing in the ocean preyed on Orcas, whereas they would eat anything and everything large enough to satisfy their considerable appetites. Even though there are much larger whales, they all live in fear of hungry Orcas hunting together in packs.

He wondered briefly whether or not he had enough speed and stamina to get away from them now that he had recovered from his earlier deep diving efforts. His inner voice provided the answer - this is not the time to try Boji!

He reached out ahead with his sonar and received many familiar responses. They were heading for his home pod. He clicked and whistled out his own sound signature as they drew closer and was delighted to recognise one of them as Ananda's. His father had not visited for many months now and his presence encouraged Boji.

What he did find strange was that they were not fleeing from the Orcas as he would have anticipated. Clearly Boji and his escorts were expected.

Nine dolphins were waiting for them - the expanded home pod of eight, not counting himself, and his father. They were all very still in the water as the Orcas slowed to a halt in front of his parents. Nevina and Ananda were very close together, tail flukes touching, and there was an air of solemnity about them which was new to Boji .

They acknowledged the Orcas, and the senior bull responded.

'The debt is paid.'

Then Boji's awesome escorts left him and disappeared back toward the open sea.

He looped to the surface, took two breaths and relaxed from the state of readiness which had held him since the appearance of the Orcas.

'That must have been some favour your were owed.' Boji beamed at his parents.

Ananda responded. 'A matter of assisting a stranded calf some years ago, but that is no longer important Boji.'

'Then what is? Why did you have me brought here?'

'Because it is time for you to make a choice my son.' Ananda continued. 'We live a simple life. We are coastal dolphins, and the essence of our survival is the support we give each other. You cannot be relied upon as a member of your home pod as you spend so much time away on your own. Though you are old enough now you don't seem to want to join another pod like mine. There is much feeling against you Boji. In many ways you are different from what is wanted or expected among us. Now the goodwill is exhausted. This is a final gesture, the last opportunity for you to choose the kind of life we dolphins lead normally, and take your place in an established pod. The alternative will be a solitary life, as any pod must be sure of your continuing presence to give support when it is needed. Many are in favour of your future non-acceptance, but your mother and I persuaded them to give you this choice. The decision is yours my son.'

Even before his father had finished Boji knew what he had to do.

If being part of a pod meant he had to give up his greatest joy - the quest arising out of his passion for learning and knowing - then his choice was clear. He felt sad that it all had to be so final, separating him from those he loved, but deep inside he was calm and determined.

'We must have an answer,' asserted one of Nevina's companions in home pod.

'I am grateful for the chance to choose.' Boji began. 'Given such a clear choice I find I must be as true to myself as I know how. I have no desire to be part of any pod which cannot accept my search, and what the results of that quest can bring to the pod. I will go my own way, in love.'

With that he moved to his parents, stroking them lightly along their flanks with his fins. Then he turned away with a last look into their eyes, and swam back toward deep water, his heart full.

TWELVE

Boji the Blue Dolphin got used to spending his life alone. Solitude was not a threat to him. Most of the time he preferred it to the company of those who refused to see, or even look at the possibilities before them.

Just occasionally he missed home pod, and then his aloneness turned to loneliness for a while.

His learning continued, and that made him happy.

No longer attached to the stretch of shoreline frequented by home pod, he travelled far.

He encountered new conditions.

Moods of the sea he had never experienced before.

Changes in temperature, of the water and of the air above it.

Different fish became part of his diet. He discovered that his deep dives brought some very tasty species within his reach.

He learned to sleep on the move, putting half his brain into a deep restful state, whilst the other half kept him breathing.

With increasing awareness and control of the energy and power available to him he dived to even greater depths, savouring the utter peace to be found there. Insights and realisations came to him in abundance in deep water when he allowed himself the luxury of simply noticing and accepting the survival messages his mind would shout at him. Instead of compulsively following their dictates he found himself playing the game of choice more and more. Sometimes he would respond to a need and turn it into what he wanted anyway. At other times he knew exactly what he wanted to do, and let the need bang away at the door of his consciousness unheeded.

What his deep dives gave him most powerfully was a sense of the oneness of everything. He came to know and recognise blissful moments when he experienced being part of every fish, every creature in the sea, every rock, every grain of sand on the sea bed - and their being part of him.

He kept alive his innate capacity for play with other sea mammals. The seals and sea lions were great fun. Most of the larger whales weren't interested, but at times they would let their calves cavort with him.

He experimented with his sonar, becoming expert at scanning the internal workings, not only of his prey, but of many other living things which crossed his path.

Boji still felt deep sadness and regret when he had the thought that he could be sharing all his discoveries with the rest of his dolphin family. Yet he knew in his heart he was fulfilling his destiny by being true to himself, and was not sorry for the price he had paid.

Boji had discovered that living a life driven by safety and survival was to be driven by fear; and his search had revealed enough of his own fear for him to know he was motivated by the greater power of love, and the boundaries opened by that discovery were limitless!

THIRTEEN

In his sixth year Boji encountered humankind directly in his environment for the first time.

In his wanderings boats of all shapes and sizes had become familiar. His repertoire of sonar echoes expanded to include all the various materials which formed the hulls of anything from small inflatables and dinghies up to ocean going liners and tankers.

He enjoyed riding the bow waves of many craft, particularly the big ones, although the first tanker he had come across had scared him initially. That meeting had prompted disbelief. His distant sonar detected this very large object moving slowly through the water. He approached warily, much as he had reacted to the Sperm Whales years before. It was at least twenty times the length of a large Sperm Whale, but he realised, with some relief, that this monster was not living tissue. The density of the steel plating he had recognised many times elsewhere but never on a vessel so large. He trusted his own speed and manoeuvrability over any of the boats he had met, so he soon discovered the delights of being pushed along ahead of this huge mass in the water.

He was aware that all these craft were directed and controlled by intelligent terrestrials wishing to extend their conditions of life over the sea. His interest thus far had been restricted to their vehicles of passage. Their boats were extra playthings, challenges to his capacity for creative play.

Boji's appearance seemed to provoke a lot of excitement among the occupants of many boats, which he found strange. He warmed to them, but it was still the boats and their movements which held his attention. That is until one big white painted liner he had been playing around slowed to a halt in the warm, crystal clear waters close to a small island.

He looped through the surface to blow, lifting his head higher so his eyes cleared the water. He saw that, apart from a knot of people at the stern of the ship, nothing much seemed to be happening. Then the anchor and chain went down from the bow. Boji was pleased. He loved the metallic sounds which came from anchor chains as the links moved with the sea. Small anchors in soft sand he could dislodge and watch fascinated as they dragged and held again, totally unaware of the mayhem he was creating aboard the boats involved. However, the anchor this ship had released was much too big for those games.

As he watched, part of the stern seemed to break away, pivoting down near the waterline. A rectangular framework was lowered until it settled on the water to enclose a small area of the surface. Some of the people at the stern were clambering down and arranging themselves on the now horizontal deck of the floating structure.

'Hey did you see the porpoise?'

'I believe it's a dolphin sir.'

'Well, whatever it is, aren't they supposed to keep sharks away?'

'It has been known, yes sir.'

'Good! I feel better about swimming then.'

Boji cruised under the stern examining the new and strange extension. Not of any great interest he decided, until suddenly the humans were jumping and diving into the water in the middle of the floating deck. He removed himself beyond the limit of visibility and proceeded to scan this new situation with his sonar. He was rivetted. Every creature he had seen or scanned in the sea was perfectly adapted to the life it led. With the exception of other whales and dolphins,

54

few of them could survive in air for very long, let alone make the cross over on to the land. He knew some turtles bred on the shore, but in doing so they must be just as clumsy and exposed as the humans seemed to be now they had forsaken their own element for the sea. They could move through the water, just, and they were clearly much more attached to the surface than he was. He moved closer. As always, he had to know.

His returning echoes were giving him a three dimensional acoustic image, so he was learning a great deal about how these creatures were built. What amazed him were the similarities with his own kind. Obviously they were air breathers adapted to live on land, and the bones of those extremities which they used to propel themselves through the water were very similar to dolphins' fins. The heart pumping warm blood around their bodies - how did they survive without a layer of blubber? Most exciting of all, he detected new young life in one of the females, and the tiny embryo could well have been a developing calf the likeness was so striking.

His mounting curiosity drew him too close.

One of the males had put a shiny cover over his eyes and trapped air against his face. He came four or five metres down, flapping his legs hard behind him. He caught sight of Boji, froze briefly, then headed frantically for the surface. Once there, bodies and legs disappeared out of the water in a few seconds.

Boji had felt the blast of fear from the adventuresome male and guessed that he had been the cause of this flurry of activity. He didn't know why but he wanted to reassure them.

Without getting too close to the stern of the ship, he leapt clear of the water three times before moving slowly around at the surface about thirty metres clear of their swimming area.

'Did you see that! Jesus, I thought it was a shark!'

'Thank you for frightening us all to death darling. Don't do it again.'

'He looks friendly.'

'Yes, but he's still very big and has a lot of teeth. I shan't be swimming again today.'

'Do you think it's alright to go in again?'

'You'll be quite safe sir. I've seen a lot of dolphins in my time. He'll do one of three things if you go back in. He could disappear completely, or cruise by at a distance so you just catch a glimpse of him occasionally, or come in close and want to play. He won't harm you.'

'I notice you're calling it 'he'. How do you know?'

'He's too big madam. The females of that species don't grow to that size. Mind you I've never seen that colour before.'

'You mean that deep blue tint?'

'That's right. He could be a one-off.'

In fact Boji was surprised at the pleasure he felt when some of the humans re-entered the water. Not as many as before, but enough for him to carry on learning about them. He was able to come into visible range for a while to add sight information to his other senses. Not wishing to frighten them again he made slow passes no closer than ten metres, and everyone seemed to be able to accept that. Indeed they seemed as interested in him now as he was in them.

Eventually the endearing bipeds got out of the water.

'Wow! That was something else. You don't know what you've missed!'

'Yes darling. Can we go now?'

The sea swimming extension folded slowly back into the ship.

A clanking noise from the bow and Boji dashed round to enjoy the sight and sounds of the anchor chain coming under stress, going vertical, rigid in the water, and finally the anchor being wrenched free.

He stayed with the liner for an hour or more, riding the bow wave, then swimming parallel with its high sides looking up at the passengers on deck with new interest. When he turned away at last his feelings were strange to him. This day's encounter with humankind was special to him and he had no idea why. He only knew he wanted to repeat the experience. Yes, they presented another opportunity for learning, but it was more than that. He had been touched by them at another level of his being. Deep memories had been stirred and a strange mix of images and feelings had surfaced. He didn't know it then, but that day's meeting was the beginning of a profound change in the course of his life.

FOURTEEN

After his meeting with the cruise ship and its passengers, Boji was drawn increasingly to the attractions of the night. The hours of darkness presented no threat to him. His sonar operated effectively twenty four hours a day, and his deep dives had made him familiar with the black depths. As the night enveloped the ocean, Boji's preference was to be resting quietly, just beneath the surface and in sight of land.

The disappearance of one bright orb into the sea at sunset, and the emergence of another in the night sky took more of his attention. They were so different. The one he could not look at directly unless it was very low on the horizon. The other only ever either white or grey, with extraordinary changes of shape.

One night when the moon was full in a clear sky, Boji found he was restless, not wanting to follow his usual pattern. He broke the surface, and instead of looping down again, he hung there, head to one side, looking up at the moon. The brightness and perfection of shape held him, and there was something more. His restlessness left him. He had an urge to breathe and he gave in to it, breathing continually and completing the cycle much slower than normal. The moon seemed to be getting larger. He felt odd - very light and deeply relaxed at the same time. The moment came when the moon filled the sky, and he was part of it! For a split second he saw himself still hanging there, then everything changed. It was no longer night but glorious day, and he was moving easily through warm, clear water with exceptional visibility. He could see for hundreds of metres in every direction. The sea was somehow finer than before, swimming was like being caressed by the water.

He thought, isn't it time I took a breath, looked up, and the surface was reflecting the most beautiful sunlight he had ever seen - it was alive. It made everything around him stand out in brilliant clarity. Drifting leisurely up to that inviting sheen of light, he blew and breathed deeply. The air was so sweet.

He tried a tentative sonar transmission, and immediately received a wealth of returning echoes which told him of the richness and abundance of life around him in this new environment.

He felt full of energy, yet it was an energy with special gifts. Deep and profound peace filled him, accompanied by a knowing that everything here in this place was exactly as it should be. Every creature, every plant, every rock, every grain of sand was expressing perfectly the same beauty, the same love that he was. He was awed by the exchange of this perfect energy with everything about him.

Several dolphins passed him in close knit pods. Everyone greeted him warmly, and he had the distinct feeling he was known to all of them. Not only that, he was accepted, liked, and the life he was leading was approved. This was unusual indeed. His experiences of his own kind so far were very different and he was deeply moved.

Everything was so vivid. Colours more intense. Life more vital. For all that a dreamlike quality pervaded every part of this reality. Boji felt completely out of control, as if different tableaus were being presented to him for a purpose, and all he had to do was be there and observe. It seemed he was in the care and control of a benevolent force greater than himself - similar to the feelings he had in early life when he never left his mother's side.

Boji was surprised when humans appeared in the waters of this reality. He hadn't expected this alien presence, yet again he felt strangely drawn to them. A group of about ten men, women and children were in visual range. Remembering what happened with the swimmers off the back of the cruise ship, he approached with caution. This time fear was absent, indeed not one of them showed any interest in him at all. Their attention was elsewhere, and the focus of it was on the opposite side of the group from his approach.

He felt intense joy and excitement in the water emanating from the humans as he swam past them at a distance to bring his senses to bear on the object of their attention.

His sonar and his sight told him simultaneously that it was another dolphin, and it was a bottlenose dolphin, like himself, even to the blue tinge in the grey of its upper body. That was another surprise. He had never seen his colouring on another dolphin before.

The other dolphin and the humans were totally absorbed with each other. Boji saw that the dolphin's body language changed slightly with each person. Very close and gentle with the children bobbing up and down, even pushing them slowly through the water with their hands on its beak. Boisterous with the adult males at the surface, leaping and breaching alongside them. Different again with one of the women who dived down to spend a few moments with him away from the others.

Boji slid through the surface and stayed head up, listening. He could hear the excited chatter and squeals of delight.

'Look Mum, he's giving me a ride!'

'Did you see that! He went right over the top of me!'

'I wish I could stay down there with him forever.'

Boji moved in closer. Still no reaction, he might have been invisible. This was another learning situation for him, that was clear, but he hadn't got the lesson yet. Then the dolphin beamed out its own sound signature at the humans, and everything fell into place. That was his own sound! He was watching himself.

In this dream he was being allowed to see himself interacting with humankind - and he liked what he saw and felt. There was a wonderful exchange of energy going on, and in this reality it was plain to see. Bringing all his enhanced senses to bear he knew changes were taking place at various levels in all concerned. It was a celebration of life which was bringing to everyone, his perceived self included, just exactly what they needed at that time.

Boji wondered if this was to be his destiny - had he been allowed to see what lay in store for him?

As thoughts tumbled through his mind the light started to fade from the sea around him. The beautiful colours and images wavered and dulled. The humans and vision of himself with them both disappeared. The moon replaced the sun and, with a shudder, Boji found himself at the surface again at night, bathed in moonshine. The need to breathe continually asserted itself momentarily, then his breathing patterns quickly returned to normal.

The Dreamtime he had come from had been so striking, an enhanced world, that Boji drifted through the next few days and weeks in increasing sadness and confusion. He had always been happy with his lot, knowing he had made a conscious choice to live the solitary, wandering life. Now he had seen and experienced something else - another way of life - and he longed for more of it.

The Dreamtime did not return, and the weight of sadness and longing upon him became almost unbearable. The glimpse of himself had raised more questions than it had answered and the confusion forced him into thinking once again about what being true to himself really meant. When he had chosen to leave pod life years before, the issue had been clear cut. Now he was at another time of critical choice, but the alternatives were not as tangible.

Eventually, help came from an unexpected source.

FIFTEEN

Boji's encounters with the larger whales had been few and far between, and memorable. His contacts with Sperm Whales had been benign, so such meetings, though rare, were welcome. Thus it was, some two months after his Dreamtime experience, that Boji exchanged sonar greetings with a large Sperm Whale swimming over deep water on its own. Normally these great whales, if they answered at all, would go on their way, but this one seemed to be heading in his direction. There was no reason to fear this creature, the largest of the toothed whales, so Boji took no avoiding action.

After several minutes, the biggest Sperm Whale Boji had seen came into view and drifted to a halt within a few metres of him. The bull whale was over twenty metres long and covered with scars, most of them circular ones from the suckers on the tentacles of giant squid he had fought. He was clearly of great age and interested in Boji, who waited and wondered.

'I am Mulata, and I too have been in the Dreamtime. That connection has drawn me to you Boji.'

This magnificent being held an image in his huge brain of part of Boji's Dreamtime experience to back up his communication. Boji received enough of it to reassure him.

'Your longing is deep and heartfelt. I am here to tell you that you may return to that place whenever you need, provided your desire is not to escape from your life here, only to enhance it. You will learn that it is part of you and can be taken with you wherever you go. Seek the moon, feel the rhythm of the waters, use the breath as you did, and you can return to learn the next lesson of the Dreamtime.'

Boji received these thoughts with a sense of awe and

63

wonder that this wise old being should seek him out. He felt bathed in the benevolent power and immense love emanating from Mulata.

As this communication sunk in, Boji could feel the sadness lifting from him. Relief flooded through him. A question started to form in his mind to clear his confusion about what he had seen.

'Yes Boji, bringer of balance, you did see something of your destiny. You are not always to be alone, but your companions will not be of your own kind. You will be fulfilled never fear, for your role is shared and enjoyed by very few. You are to be a carrier, a bringer of messages to humankind of their progress. Learning and expanding your horizons have always been precious to you and your fulfilment will come from learning the many ways of conveying your messages.'

With that, Mulata moved his tail flukes and his great bulk slowly disappeared from view. Boji beamed out his thanks and his own sound signature. There was a single deep response like a thunderclap, and Mulata was gone.

SIXTEEN

Boji's vigour and zest for life returned. As a result of his encounter with the considerable presence of the old whale, his curiosity about humankind increased. He had always liked playing around their boats, and now his interest in the creatures who controlled them, fed by his deep desire to learn, became a priority. Coastal waters attracted him again as the human presence was more in evidence in shallower waters. He had hours of fun cavorting around the larger ships, but he realised that the bigger the hull in the water, the more distant were the people on board by virtue of their height from the surface. The smaller boats were his favourites, they made it easier to observe those on board and to discern their reactions to him.

One exception to this favouritism came when he spent the best part of a stormy day exploring a deep water inlet. He followed a channel carved from the sea bed between two steep headlands, which proved to be the only access to a large area of water almost enclosed by the land. He tasted the decreasing levels of salt in the water and became alert to the probability of a good meal of fish different from his usual prey. It seemed these waters were fed liberally by streams and rivers of freshwater off the land.

Before he had time to feed however, his attention was taken by the hull of a ship picking up speed toward the opening he had just entered. He was intrigued. The shape of this monster was new to him. Although it was travelling at the surface, most of its cylindrical bulk seemed to be under the water. It even had a large, flat metal tail.

As it drew closer he moved to one side, and keeping his distance, swam parallel with this unusual vessel.

It's as if they have tried to build a larger than life whale, Boji thought.

He blew and spy-hopped at the same time, holding his head vertically out of the water. He caught sight of what looked like a huge square dorsal fin with one or two humans right at the top of it. He thought, if that dorsal fin was a different shape I could be looking at a copy of an Orca, only ten times the size.

The great machine churned its way out between the headlands into the open sea. Boji became bolder. He could not perceive any threat to him so he moved in, keeping station with the strange craft alongside, then off the stern, beneath the keel, and finally bow riding.

Just as he was starting to enjoy himself, he received a shock to his confidence and his ideas about humans. This huge, mechanical Orca slowly, majestically, and obviously under control, submerged beneath him. He fled, this was too much.

Within five minutes his curiosity had got the better of him and he was back to four hundred metres range busily scanning this new development. The thing had levelled out at a depth of no more than fifty metres.

He approached it again. Soon he was taking delight in the biggest man made plaything he had experienced in his own environment. Yes, he had toyed with anchors and their chains, a few lobster pots, and swum around many wrecks of ships clearly designed to stay on the surface, but this was different. This ship was meant to be down there in his world. For once, he could examine every part of a human craft, and he spent a long time cruising just above the upper surfaces, particularly the dorsal fin where he had seen people standing before the thing submerged.

He enjoyed himself around this huge, metallic, dumb

66

whale for over an hour. Then he was hit by a simple, crude sonar transmission. Oh! Perhaps not so dumb, he thought, but they won't learn much about me from that sound. It kept coming and he knew this ship, or rather its controllers, would have located him, but that was about all.

Tiring of his games with this new toy, he slowed and let it move ahead. His last view of it was the screw spinning soundlessly beneath the imitation tail flukes as it disappeared into the murk.

He continued to sonar it for several minutes, then satisfied at last with what he had gained from this meeting, he let it go. He vowed to himself to be on the alert for such craft, it would be fun to meet one in really deep water to see what it could do.

What amused and touched him were the obvious signs to him that humankind seemed to be willing to learn from his kind about what worked in the sea. The shape, manoeuvrability, speed, and sonar they used were all crude, but created at least a semblance of what the real whales and dolphins could do.

SEVENTEEN

Feeding himself had never been a problem for Boji. Since his father had assisted him years before in the use and direction of his sonar as a feeding aid he had rarely gone hungry.

Spending more time in coastal waters gave him access to the fishing boats which could provide him with an easy meal. Some of them trawled nets behind them for several kilometres at a time. The catches varied, and Boji found that if he cruised along behind the net, or by its open maw, there were always a few fish to be had. With the humans' unwitting assistance like this, he could even feed in clearer waters on sight alone.

Where fish were plentiful, he returned the compliment whenever he could. If he came upon a trawler with its nets up on the stern ready, sailing over a barren sea, Boji would sonar in every direction for a shoal of fish. Locating one, he would surface and try and make his presence felt by leaping and breaching in full view of the boat, then dashing away in the direction of the shoal. He knew when he had been seen, but only once every so often would the skipper realise what was going on and follow him.

One early summer morning off a sub-tropical shore he greeted a smaller boat with nets piled untidily at the stern. He could not direct them to fish as there were few about. He was one hundred metres or so from the boat, and as he blew he was close enough to hear the excited chatter and see the flurry of movement at his arrival.

Then, once more, Boji was confronted by the unknown.

He saw one of the men point at him with something longer than the man's arm. There was a sharp crack, a puff of smoke, and a hole appeared right through Boji's dorsal fin. He felt the shock of the impact and instinctively looped downward. A second shot rang out and Boji was hit high in the body, behind his dorsal fin.

'Got him! That'll teach him.'

'Well done. Him and his kind are putting us out of business. No wonder there are no fish if there are dolphins around.'

'Yeah. I'd rather see sharks than dolphins - at least they only take the fish that are sick and dying. The dolphins gorge themselves on the good fish that we should be catching.'

Boji dived to the sea bed and swam fast away from the boat toward deeper water for several minutes.

The only physical pain ever inflicted on him had been the raking by his peers' teeth when they didn't want him around. That was superficial and momentary. This was different. Once the initial numbness from the impact wore off, he began to hurt as he had never hurt before. He was hardly aware of the wound to his dorsal fin, just a slight soreness. The pain from the second bullet still in his body was deep and persistent. Every movement of his tail flukes sent a searing reminder of the bullet's presence through him. Stillness merely changed the quality of the pain without reducing its intensity.

The hours of enduring this unwanted new experience were relieved only by moments of surrender. When he was able to give up totally to the presence of the pain in his body and let it be there, he knew times of blissful relief, even pleasure. But these were short-lived, as soon as he became goal oriented again, chasing his prey, or even heading upward for his next breath, the moment was gone and his agony reasserted its hold.

The hours became days and, as he attempted to lead his normal life, exploring, feeding, playing - he was giving boats a miss for the time being - he imagined that the pain was reducing. What he didn't realise was the tissue at the surface of the wound was joining and healing for a while, only to be opened again from beneath by the rotting flesh around the embedded bullet. He was losing feeling at the site of the wound as nerve ends were destroyed. Toxins circulated within him, producing a lassitude which was new to him. He was used to having lots of energy. Lack of it changed him. He moved around much less. More time was spent at the surface just breathing and lowering himself a metre or so and hanging in the water. An ugly circle of white pulpy tissue marred the blue/grey sheen of his upper body. Tiny fish, emboldened by his lack of response, picked at the dead flesh around the wound.

The vitality, the love of life as a wonderful adventure to be enjoyed, a game to be played, all so evident in a dolphin, faded from Boji. His body was becoming a burden to him instead of a superb vehicle for the expression of how it is to be a dolphin.

As that burden became heavier, another impulse grew in strength.

Dolphins and whales have a response to an unfavourable situation which, in extremis, becomes a conscious choice to let go the body, a 'time to die' decision. In the wild, strandings are the result of such a choice, and Boji felt the pull toward shallow water. A vision of a beach with the sea bed shelving rapidly up to it kept appearing in his mind, and it became increasingly attractive.

He drifted along a busy coastline, not seeking boats now, on the contrary, looking for a haven with the minimum of activity close inshore. Not easy to find, the warm waters in the area were popular with humankind. All the time Boji's 'time to die' drive was crystallising into something which felt compulsive and final.

Eventually his dulled senses perceived a desolate beach, backed by sand dunes, with a headland defining one end. His discovery was made at low tide so he knew he had some time to wait before fulfilling his now overwhelming drive to leave his pain-wracked body behind.

Images from the past floated across his fevered mind. Early times with his mother Nevina, and his father Ananda. Visions of the Dreamtime and Mulata the Great Sperm Whale troubled him, for he remembered vaguely something about his destiny being different from what now seemed inevitable.

Fish becoming more plentiful around him reminded him that the tide was approaching its height. He swam slowly into water less than a metre deep and waited for the right wave. Several washed over his back before one lifted him as he wanted. With the surge of water assisting him, he used what remained of his strength to drive himself through the shallows. The big wave retreated to leave him with his belly on the sand and water lapping at the lower half of his body.

Boji the Blue Dolphin had beached himself.

EIGHTEEN

Dusk followed that high tide. Boji was dimly aware of different realities as darkness came quickly to that lonely beach. When he was in present time his weight and immobility out of the water seemed to exaggerate the pain and the burden of his body. With his eyes closed, other times and places overcame him, seducing him away from his plight.

The air temperature had dropped considerably and the night air was very humid, so the damaging process of his skin drying in air was slowed to a minimum. His breathing rate became irregular, with longer and longer intervals between each exchange. He had the ability to stop breathing and die as a voluntary decision, yet with his brain literally intoxicated, it never occurred to him to do so. He simply waited to die.

The illusions persisted. They centred around his breathing. As the periods between each breath came close to being life threatening, visions of dolphins and whales known and unknown urged him to breathe. Mulata appeared more than most, with great power and clarity his voice vibrated through Boji.

'Breathe Blue Dolphin, breathe!'

Crabs, the shoreline foragers of the night, emerged from the rock pools under the headland. Normally they depended for their food on much smaller creatures being washed up dead on their beach. On this night the prospect of a greater prize attracted them to Boji in scores. Their explorations of his body told them that most of him was still living tissue. Then some of the bolder, or hungrier, crabs discovered the wound in his side and the dead flesh around it. Sometimes

Boji became aware of them and managed a weak shudder or flick of his tail flukes, but only discouraged them for a moment or two.

Piece by tiny piece, the rotting tissue was picked away by small, precise crustacean pincers and jaws to leave a deep crater which marred the smooth shape of Boji's body.

As the sky lightened again most of the crabs scuttled back to the safety and relative coolness of their home rocks and pools. A few of the smaller ones lingered to take their chances on what little remained for them. Much of what was now exposed was healthy, living tissue and not to their taste. It didn't matter. What did matter was that the crabs who had dined on Boji that night helped to save his life.

NINETEEN

'Steven! Steven! Don't run too far ahead of us. We've never been along here before.'

'Don't worry Mum. I'll stay in sight of you.'

'Make sure you do.'

This holiday was different. Of necessity, the Winch family, John, Sarah, and son Steven, had taken holidays close to home since Steven's birth. This year there had been a breakthrough in their finances and they had been able to travel much further afield.

Steven was in heaven. He had never seen beaches so clean and water so clear. He loved the water, taking after his mother in that respect. So, with his non-swimming father outvoted, most days were spent in finding new beaches to enjoy.

Wherever the roads with good surfaces existed along the coast, the beaches were well populated. As the roads petered out and became rough tracks, and finally just footpaths, the small coves and bays emerged devoid of human presence.

The Winches had given way to Steven's urging to find somewhere they could have to themselves. Even at ten years old he knew he loved the space and freedom of an empty or near empty beach over a crowded one. His father had taken the car as far as he could and had left it where the gravel beneath the tyres had finally given way to soft sand.

After a lengthy walk, Steven discovered the delights of playing in sand dunes. He clambered up the side of a mound which dwarfed him, loving the feel of the sand on his feet and legs. Arriving breathless at the top, he caught sight of the sea three or four hundred metres away before he let himself tumble and roll down the seaward side of the dune. He felt safe in the sand. He could throw himself around almost as much as he did in the water without hurting himself.

He launched himself from the top of the next dune, dropping four or five metres before the sloping loose sand absorbed his fall in a great golden splash. Rolling over into the valley between two dunes he sat up and listened. He heard his mother calling again, so he climbed to the top of another dune and waited for his parents to come into view. He stayed with them and, after what seemed an age to Steven, the family came down the slope of the last dune before the sand flattened out to a gentle gradient down to the water's edge.

'What's that?' exclaimed Steven.

'What's what?'

'Look over there, not far from the rocks. Oh, come on Dad!'

'Take it easy. It could be a dead shark, or even worse, a live one!'

'Steven, stay with us. We look at it together, or not at all.'

It was all the boy could do to contain himself and approach Boji slowly in company with his parents. As they did, the last of the crabs dropped from Boji's body and hurried away over the hard, wet sand.

'Ugh, how disgusting. Did you see that?'

'The poor thing must be dead.'

As if in answer, Boji breathed out weakly and took a shallow in-breath.

'Oh my God! It's a dolphin and it's still alive. It's stranded.'

'I wonder how long he's been here,' said Steven, 'his skin looks awful - all blotchy.'

'You don't know if it's a he or a she Steven,' said his mother.

'I know, but I don't feel right calling the dolphin 'it',' said Steven staunchly.

They were standing two metres away from Boji on his right side. Steven moved in closer, pulling against his mother's restraining hand on his shoulder.

'What were the crabs doing if he's still alive?'said John Winch.

And then they saw the ghastly wound on the left side of Boji's body just behind his dorsal fin.

'That's what they were after.' John answered his own question.

'God, that hole must be four inches across and the same deep.'

'Don't you mean ten centimetres Dad?'

'Yes, alright son.'

'What could have caused such an injury?' asked Sarah.

'A boat's propeller perhaps. No, it's the wrong shape for that.'

Steven had been edging his way closer all the time.

'Be careful!' warned his mother.

'It's O.K. Mum. We had this chap giving a talk about dolphins at school last term. He said that dolphins in the wild never hurt humans.'

Steven was peering closely at the hole in Boji's side.

'Hey, look at this Dad. Is that a bullet in him?'

'I think you're right.'

A small dark circle of metal could just be seen deep in the middle of the exposed tissue.

'The crabs must have opened it up.'

'Can we help him Dad - please?'

'Well, I don't know. I suppose we should call the Authorities in this area - police or coast guard - people like that.'

'But that'll take too long. He'll die!'

John and Sarah Winch looked at each other. Sarah gave her husband an encouraging smile and a slight nod of her head.

'Alright, let's see what we can do. Steve, have you got your bucket with you?'

'Yes. It's in Mum's bag.'

'O.K. It will be your job to keep him wet. The sun is getting hotter every moment and his skin is already drying out. So, go backwards and forwards to the sea with your bucket and keep pouring water over him, but not down his blowhole.'

'What can I do?' asked Sarah. 'He'll need shade won't he?'

'Drape one of the towels over his body, and Steve can keep the towel wet. Use your own body and the other towel to give him as much shade as possible. I'm going back to the car. In my tool kit I've got a pair of long-nosed pliers. They might be just the thing to get that bullet out.'

With that Steven's father turned and jogged up the beach.

'I'll be back as soon as I can,' he shouted over his shoulder.

Sarah used the two big beach towels she had brought just as John had suggested.

Steven dashed off down the beach, and returned with his bucket half empty. In his excitement he'd lost a lot of water running back to Boji. Even so they were both rewarded and encouraged by a feeble flip of his tail and another breath as the first precious half bucket was tipped over the site of the wound. Steven learned to pace himself better, and much more water went where it was intended in the next half hour.

They petted and talked to Boji constantly, only stroking thoroughly wetted skin. At intervals they swopped roles and Steven would do the shading, and Sarah the water carrying.

A strange and subtle bonding came about which affected all three of them.

Something very deep in Boji responded, not only to the care and affection he was receiving, but also to the people themselves. In his clearer moments he wanted to communicate with them, and did so the only way he could in his predicament - with small body signals - a shudder, the opening or closing of an eyelid, the flick of a tail fluke. Each time he felt the response on an emotional level as well as hearing the delighted noises they made.

At last John Winch returned, breathing heavily, clutching a bundle which he dropped on the sand next to Boji. Steven had never been so pleased to see his father, and Sarah hugged him as if he had been away for a week.

'Wow! I must do that more often if that's the kind of welcome I get! Here, let me hold the towel for a bit while I calm down, that was a long run!'

After a minute or two, John said 'You two have done well - he's good and wet, his skin looks better, and he's opening his eyes more often - great! Now let's see if we can remove that bullet, if that's what it is. If it's a small harpoon head, or anything with a barb on it, we're in trouble.'

He opened the bundle on the sand, and there were the long-nosed pliers, and a quarter bottle of whisky. Sarah looked at him.

'Where did you get that?'

'It's not as bad as it looks. I always carry some whisky in the car for a little dutch courage when I have to give an important presentation at work.'

'Well. That's something else I've learned today.' Sarah breathed.

'Come on Dad,' urged Steven.

'Right, here we go.'

John cleaned the pliers as best he could with a cloth from his bundle, and then poured some of the whisky over the long tapering jaws of the precious tool.

Sarah moved to shade her husband's body, and Steven was ready with more sea water.

John reached in to the depths of the wound until he felt the touch of metal on metal. Opening the jaws of the pliers, he gritted his teeth and pushed the pliers gently into the flesh on either side of the alien metal. Boji didn't move, but a short, sharp squeal of pain burst from his blowhole. Steven's father closed the pliers on the circle of metal. Taking a firm grip with both hands, he tried a steady, firm pull. Nothing happened. He relaxed, retaining his hold on the pliers.

'What I need is a pull the other way. Sarah, leave the towel and get on the other side of his body from me. That's it. Now put your hands on either side of the wound and when I try again, you pull your way and resist me.'

He was sweating profusely. Wiping his face on his upper arms, he took a deep breath and tried again. He nodded to Sarah to hold Boji's body against the pull of his efforts.

This time, when he was sure the pliers' jaws were as tight as he could get them, he pulled and twisted at the same time.

There was a horrid sucking noise and the bullet came free. John fell backwards still holding on tight to the pliers.

'Got it!' he yelled, as Boji screamed again in the agony of the moment.

Briefly, the Winch family went berserk. They jumped around on the sand, hugging each other and whooping with delight.

Steven was the first back to Boji. A trickle of blood came from the hole left by the bullet. A serious blood flow they couldn't have done much about, and this trickle, already lessening, was a good sign.

'Yes Steven,' said Sarah, 'pour some more water over the wound, the sea water is a saline solution which will help healing anyway.'

Steven wasn't sure what a saline solution was, but he didn't care. He wanted so much to help this creature he had already taken to his heart, he was happy to do as he was told.

'What now?' asked Sarah, 'The three of us will never get him back into the water on our own, he's much too big.'

'It's alright,' said John, 'help is on the way. I went down to a beach close to where I left the car. There were six or seven families and a bunch of teenagers. I told one young couple we were trying to help a stranded dolphin and the word spread like wildfire. Within about five minutes I had people all round me wanting to help. It was amazing. I gave them an idea of his size and told them we would need a sling of some sort, like a large stretcher, and a lot of muscle. I think there's a small army on its way here!'

The Winches went back to shading and wetting Boji, murmuring encouragement and stroking him gently.

The pain had played its part in bringing Boji back from the brink. He was more aware of what was happening than at any time since he beached himself.

After a while they heard shouts of greeting coming from the sand dunes, and about twenty people emerged from them. As soon as they saw Boji, some of the younger ones came running down the beach. John went to meet them.

'Easy, easy. We don't want to scare him,' he said.

The noise and the shouts softened as they all came close and gathered round.

John and Steven were relieved to see two men behind everyone else walking steadily down the beach carrying what could be a makeshift stretcher.

Sarah was busy talking into Boji's left ear, or at least where she imagined it would be if he had an ear.

'Everything's going to be fine. We'll have you back in the water soon.'

When everyone had arrived, John told them what had happened so far and what he proposed to do with their help. There were nods of agreement.

'O.K. Let's have a look at his transport.'

In the time available they had done well. A large piece of canvas had been looped around two long oars from an old open fishing boat. Odd lengths of rope had been threaded through holes punched along the edges of the canvas and tied where they met down the outside of one of the oars. The stretch of canvas available to Boji was about a metre across and four metres long. The oars projected at least a metre beyond the canvas to form four handles for this crude but effective stretcher.

When this was in place on the sand down by Boji's right side, John instructed his son.

'Steve, can you make sure the canvas is wet and as free as possible of sand and anything else which might damage his skin.'

'O.K. Dad.'

'Right. Could I have five of you who are reasonably fit and strong please?'

Four men and one woman came forward. When they were spread evenly along Boji's left side, they squatted down, following John's lead, with their hands against the top half of Boji's body. John had his hands either side of the bullet wound.

'What we need is a steady push, building up slowly until he topples on to the stretcher on his right side.'

'What about his flipper Dad?'

'Good for you son. I'd forgotten about that. Before we start, see if you can tuck it tight against his body.'

Steven was relieved that Boji did not resist as his right fin was pulled back gently but firmly along his body.

'Let's try it first, just to feel his weight.'

Boji chose that moment to breathe again, and two of the team near his head jumped and let go, returning red-faced to the task a moment later.

'Come on, start to push, get used to his bulk.'

'My God, he's heavy!'

Boji's underbelly had just started to lift free of the sand when they let him down again.

'We could do with some more hands.'

Room was made for two more willing helpers.

'Now, this time, after three - one, two, three - heave!'

Boji's body lifted off the sand down his left side, passed the point of no return, rolled over the nearside oar, and flopped on the canvas on his right side. He had never felt so powerless, so out of control. Yet he knew he was among friends and he had long since surrendered to whatever was happening.

An involuntary cheer went up.

'Yes!' 'Great!' 'Well done!'

'Now we need as many as we can get on the ends of those oars to carry him to the water. The eight fittest first please, no back problems! Two on each corner, and then anyone who can find a space on the oars join in! Remember to lift with your legs, not your back.'

A moment or two of confusion, then everyone was in place.

'Here we go. One - two - three - lift!'

And up he came. The canvas sagged, the oars bowed, but the makeshift stretcher held.

Boji was completely disoriented by these strange sensations. He was just grateful for the water being poured over him. The sun was high in the sky now, and very hot.

The sea was in mid-tide and not too far away. Even so they had to put him down once for a rest before feeling the water lapping around their feet. The sand shelved quickly, and within a few more steps the exhausted carriers were up to their thighs and Boji's weight in the water was getting less.

'A little further,' gasped John, 'then we can try and take the canvas from under him.'

In fact, the rest was easy.

As Boji felt the support of the water, he righted himself, took a breath and remained at the surface while his human rescuers pushed the stretcher down beneath him, collapsed it, and let it float slowly up again to one side of him.

Boji hung motionless. Everyone had their eyes glued to him while they recovered from their efforts.

Someone said 'Supposing he beaches himself again. Don't they do that sometimes when they've been rescued?'

The main fear of the little group had been voiced.

John felt Boji's next move would be critical. If he turned and made toward the shore again, all their efforts would have been for nothing. If he moved toward the open sea it would all have been worth it.

Boji felt something fundamental had changed within him. He was still in pain, and there was a different quality about it. The 'time to die' syndrome had gone. He was glad to be back in his own environment.

He turned slowly, and with barely discernible movements of his tail flukes, swam among the creatures who were so unpredictable. One of their kind had shot him, and yet here were several more who had saved his life.

The Winches came together in waist deep water, arms

around each other, tears streaming down their sunburnt faces. Steven could hardly speak.

'Is he going to be alright?' he whispered.

'I don't know. We've done all we can for him. It's up to him now.' His mother responded.

Boji sought them out and drifted up to circle them. They each reached out to him, to stroke him just one more time.

'Oh look John. I'm sure he's saying 'Thank you' to us.'

Steven whispered 'Goodbye. We love you,' and buried his face in his mother's arms.

Boji headed out into the bay, away from his human friends.

He didn't hear the demented cheering and shouting that broke out among the volatile bipeds in the shallows.

TWENTY

As it turned out, Steven's goodbye was premature. The day after their dramatic rescue, the Winches wanted nothing more than to collapse in a heap in the shade somewhere. Steven managed to persuade them that they could do that on the same remote beach as their previous day's adventure.

As they came over the sand dunes again, John half expected to see the dolphin on the beach. As Steven raced away from them down the last soft slope, his father breathed a sigh of relief at the sight of the empty stretch of sand.

'Thank God. He's not re-beached himself.'

'I was worried about that too. Steven would have been heartbroken.'

Steven stood at the water's edge peering out into the bay. If you're there, please let me see you, he thought.

Several minutes passed, and then as if in answer, a dark dorsal fin broke the surface and was gone again about two hundred metres from the shore.

'He's here! He's here!' he shouted, and he went racing back to where his parents had found a sheltered place to settle.

'Are you sure it's him? It could be a shark, or another dolphin.'

'No, it's not a shark Mum. Their dorsals are like triangles. Dolphins' dorsal fins look more like the thorn on a rose bush. And you don't have to worry about sharks if there are dolphins around. Least that's what the chap said who came to our school. Is it alright if I go in?'

'Yes, you can, but don't go too far out. I want to be able to see you from here.' said Sarah.

Boji was feeling very weak, but with the source of infection removed, his body's self-healing mechanisms were working well, and the pain had already softened to a dull ache when he was still.

He swam slowly, if at all. One flick of his tail had prompted a stabbing pain from the site of the wound, so he had been reminded that he was far from ready to resume normal activities. He had no wish to leave the protection of the bay for a while. The warmth and stillness of the shallow water suited him. Not surprisingly, his appetite had deserted him. Even if he had been able to catch his prey, in his convalescent state he had no desire to eat. In the warm water his body could afford to draw on the fat reserves in his blubber for sustenance.

He was delighted to find his sonar abilities unaffected by his ordeal, and amused himself getting to know the bay and its occupants in detail.

When Steven Winch ran and dived into the sea he had no idea where Boji might be.

Boji knew of his presence the moment Steven hit the water.

The boy was fearless in his excitement. He swam straight out into the centre of the bay where he had seen Boji blow a few moments before. At last Steven stopped swimming, trod water and recovered his breath. It could have been another dolphin, he thought, Mum could be right about that. No, he dismissed that possibility. In his heart he knew it was his friend from the previous day.

Boji hugged the sea bed and moved slowly in underneath Steven until the boy was seven or eight metres directly above him. From there Boji knew, visually and acoustically, that this was the young male human who had stayed at his side for the whole of his painful ordeal under the sun.

He allowed himself to drift upwards and to one side of Steven, surfacing gently about two metres from him. Even so the 'whoosh' of Boji's out breath startled Steven and a rush of fear went through him.

'It is you. I knew it! Ooh, can't you let me know you're coming, you scared me! Oh no, don't go away!'

Boji had felt the blast of fear from the boy and moved out to stop twenty metres away. From there he scanned Steven again until it was obvious the fear in him had subsided. Boji came in closer, on the surface this time.

Steven swam a few strokes toward him and reached out to touch his dorsal fin.

Boji let him do so for a few seconds then dropped down and forward so Steven had to let go.

'That bullet hole in your dorsal looks nice and clean anyway. I wish I could see your side.'

Boji could feel the vibrations in the water from Steven speaking out loud in air, without understanding. What he did pick up were brief impressions of a dorsal fin and a side view of a dolphin as Steven spoke. He was used to receiving and interpreting instantaneously a kind of three dimensional acoustic image from the echoes of his returning sonar transmissions. This was strange for the images that left fleeting impressions on his mind were visual, like a very weak version of the easy telepathy he experienced with his own kind.

Steven put his face in the water and reached for Boji's side just above the left fin.

Boji allowed the contact and moved slowly past, letting the boy's hand drift along his body until it was close to the open wound, then he deliberately arched his tail stock away.

'O.K., O.K. I get the message. I'll stay away from that awful hole in you.'

Again, Boji had a mental picture of a ghastly wound, open white flesh in a grey/blue body, and somehow he knew that was how his injury appeared to this boy.

'Hey, what shall I call you? You've got to have a name.'

Boji looped to the surface, enjoying a closeness, an intimacy with this young human he had thought impossible with any being apart from other dolphins and whales. He stayed at the surface, head tilted to one side. With one eye clear of the water he could have a good look at Steven. The boy was looking straight back at him and his face lit up. Boji was learning again, and loving every moment. He saw the expressions and the light in Steven's eyes which accompanied the joy and excitement he could feel in the water around him.

Steven noticed something new.

'You've changed colour! You're much darker than yesterday, a kind of deep blue. That's what I'll call you - Bluey!'

As Boji received the picture formed in Steven's mind as he spoke, he held an image of himself in full health and strength to reinforce Steven's conclusions.

Sarah's voice carried across the water.

'You're too far out Steven, I want you closer than that.'

He waved his assent and started a slow breast stroke toward the shore, hoping his new friend would stay with him. If he was honest with himself, he wouldn't be sorry to feel the sand under his feet again.

Boji swam beneath him until the water shelved to no more than two metres deep. Then in farewell, he released huge bubbles of air which ballooned to the surface, bursting all around the boy.

I know, thought Steven, you're going now, so am I, but I'll be back.

TWENTY ONE

All but one of the days that remained of the Winches' holiday were spent on 'Bluey's Beach', as Steven called it. Sarah was quite happy about it, in fact she often went in with her son to see the dolphin. She was still more wary of him than Steven, particularly in deep water, so Boji tended to keep his distance. Sarah got her pleasure from watching the two of them together. Steven in his innocence and trust, Boji in his returning mobility and strength responding playfully to that trust as the days went by.

John wasn't a water person so he grumbled about the journey at times, and on one exceptional day put his foot down for what he wanted 'for a change'. He had to admit though that he had never seen his son so enthusiastic about anything before and he realised that if he restricted access to Steven's new friend, he could create a rift between himself and his son at a sensitive age. Typically, he played down his part in the dolphin's rescue.

Steven's enjoyment of his relationship with the blue dolphin expanded the day he brought treasured new possessions to the beach - a face mask and snorkel tube. After a little practise with them he could lie quietly at the surface, looking down and breathing easily, without all the effort of treading water in the vertical position. Being able to see Boji clearly under the water added to the intensity of the experience. It pleased him to get a good look at Boji's side and report to his parents that the wound was healing well - the hole was smaller and the new tissue looked firm and healthy.

The greatest gift was that of eye contact. When the boy and the dolphin swam alongside each other, sometimes their speeds and body positions corresponded exactly. Steven looked with wonder into one of Boji's deep brown eyes. He felt totally loved and loving. A deep bonding took place, and when his mother asked why he emerged from the sea crying, all he could say was 'I don't know Mum. I just love him.'

The last day of the holiday was bitter sweet. Steven spent as long as he could in the water.

Boji looked forward to their playtimes together as much as the boy. He was ready to return to his wanderings and whatever was in store for him outside the bay, yet the slow dawning of communication with Steven held him in the waters familiar to them both.

On that day, Boji became very physical, rejoicing in his own body again and the trust the boy had in him. Spectacular leaps over Steven; swimming at him fast then turning at the last moment to miss him by a whisker; even tapping him lightly around the head and shoulders with his beak; all had the boy beside himself with delight.

The moment of parting had to come, and they both knew it. Boji felt the weight of Steven's sadness, and saw fleeting pictures of strange places without water, lots of people moving around, and unknown machines. Perhaps the boy was thinking of home. Boji responded with images of his own undersea home, the colours, the reefs and rocks, the fish, the kelp, and hoped Steven would take home clear memories of the beauty of it all.

Swimming for the last time back into shore together, Boji let Steven put his head against his own and put his arm around Boji's great body.

John and Sarah joined their son in the shallows to say their goodbyes.

One more brief caress of his silky smooth skin.

Then he turned, and as he moved away he tail-lobbed twice, lifting his tail flukes in the air and bringing them crashing down to drench the Winches and leave them laughing through their tears.

Boji chose to stay in the bay for another two days and nights. He didn't expect to see his young human friend again, but the place had become special to him and he was happy to be there for a little longer.

Fish of a good size were not plentiful so he ate sparingly.

He was relieved that there seemed to be no permanent damage after his ordeal. There would be an indentation and a splash of livid white scar tissue to mar the uniform colour and shape of his upper body.

Boji neither knew nor cared how he looked. His body was working again and his vitality was almost back to pre-injury levels - that's what mattered to him.

On the third morning without any sign of human company, he cruised out past the headland into the open sea. He took a good meal from a passing shoal of long, lean fast moving fish, and was pleased with his ability to catch such agile prey.

Feeling like celebrating, he breached several times, leaping high into the air and falling on his side or his back with a thunderous explosion of water.

With that he let go his painful recollections of the immediate past and headed for deep water.

TWENTY TWO

For a while Boji returned to the solitary pleasures of deep diving. The challenge was no longer there, but that didn't seem as important as it had in his earlier life. Going down into the blackness, feeling the familiar sensations of his body adjusting to the pressure, the solitude, all seemed to cleanse him. Reassurance of his return to health also came along when he achieved his old record depth of eight hundred metres with energy in reserve.

However, the attractions of the depths did not hold him for long. On the contrary, the images that came to him most when he was down there contained shallow waters and humans. His cruise ship encounter, his Dreamtime experience, Mulata's communication, and his time with Steven, filled his mind whenever he allowed himself the indulgence of contemplating the past or the future. The net effect of all this was the reinforcement of his earlier interest in humans to the level at which he felt the resurgence of a familiar longing. The longing for new experience and learning which for him, as Mulata had expressed, would find fulfilment in interaction with humankind. Those two legged land based intelligences who had, in the space of a few weeks, both endangered and saved his life.

Responding to the pull he was feeling, he returned to coastal waters seeking areas where boats were plentiful. He avoided those with nets on board. Others he played around and watched the reactions of the humans when he could see them. They seemed content to enjoy his presence from the safety of their boats for the most part. Only rarely did anyone get into the water, and then they were often cloaked in fear which prompted Boji to keep his distance.

What he could not know was that word had spread along this stretch of coast about the big blue dolphin who had been shot, stranded, and rescued. Because the Winches were not there to tell the true story of their experiences with him, stories about him had been first exaggerated, then fabricated. The result was people did not know what to believe about him. He was an unknown quantity, and the unknown always provoked a measure of fear among humans.

This went on for some weeks and Boji began to wonder if what he had found so far was to be the future pattern of his life. What he had felt and enjoyed with Steven was so different from any of the brief encounters he had had since. He tried going yet further away from the site of his rescue. Nothing changed. Many watched him from boats, even cheered and reacted strongly to his acrobatics, yet few swam and then the contact was fleeting and superficial.

He moved on, knowing he was searching, but for what? Perhaps he needed to spend a longer time in one particular place, was that what he was seeking?

Looking for answers he returned to deep water, remembering the depths had sometimes brought him profound thoughts, feelings, images. After three dives beyond five hundred metres he still had no answers, yet a clue surfaced in his inner vision as to what might provide the next step in his search.

Cruising inverted at around six hundred metres Boji was concentrating on his sonar scans, for these were unknown waters, when a clear impression of the night sky dropped into his awareness. Just as black as the surrounding sea at that depth, relieved by thousands of twinkling stars, and, larger than life, the moon - a dazzling presence in his vision.

Of course, he thought, what was it Mulata had said? He could return to the Dreamtime whenever he needed, as long as he did not seek to escape the reality of his life, only to enhance it.

What he sought was direction, he knew what he wanted to do, now he needed to know where was the best place to do it. That wasn't escape surely, that was acceptance of his place in reality.

He headed for the surface, excitement and anticipation rising within him. The blackness gave way to deep blue, then to lighter shades of the same blue as he powered his way upward. The ascent still gave him pleasure, even though the pain of oxygen starvation in deep muscle tissue told him he had been at the limit of his endurance this time. The only problem was the day was at its height, and the moon was nowhere to be seen. He had no choice but to wait for the night, and hope it would be a clear one.

In the event, that night was completely overcast, and Boji learnt some more about letting go strong emotions. About being content with himself and the fullness of the present moment.

Finally, a day and a half after his illuminating dive, he had his chance. The moon was not full as it had been before, just under half its surface was in light, so a deep crescent was presented, and Boji wondered if his entry to the Dreamtime depended upon a full moon.

He hung vertically at the surface, his eyes just clear of the water, and looked up at the beautiful shape in the heavens.

As before, he changed the rhythm of his breathing, this time letting it coincide with his imagining of the sound of waves rushing up over a pebbled shore and receding again.

Nothing changed for several minutes, then gradually, extraordinary peace filled him. As he surrendered to that the crescent moon started to fill out. Boji felt a sense of wonder at what was happening, coupled with tremendous gratitude - to what or whom he knew not.

Again the silver orb, now in all its glory, swallowed him.

Momentarily, he knew every cell in his body were as the stars in the sky before his awareness departed to another reality.

This time the water he found himself in at first was cold and murky. The feeling of being an observer rather than a participant had returned, so he gave in and trusted what he was being shown. No more than five people at the surface, all clad in a close fitting body suit, even hands and feet protected. He'd never seen that before, but he knew humans had virtually no blubber to insulate them, so these suits must be to provide them with something similar. He recognised the contraptions on their heads and the sinewy elongations to their feet. He had seen the same things on Steven and others he had met. These five people were with an adult dolphin, a bottlenose like himself, and this interaction was accompanied by very little fear.

Everyone seemed to be having fun, particularly the dolphin, who was very tactile and seemed to want nothing more than to touch the swimmers with as many parts of his anatomy as possible!

Boji was drawn upward to break the surface and look around. He saw a single boat, behind which was a small harbour entrance. A breakwater to one side created an area of calm water and a protected beach adjacent to the harbour. The surrounding landscape was relatively flat and broke up the horizon into gentle undulations of green.

Boji submerged again and swam away, certain that he was not seeing himself as he had done before.

The water changed in colour, visibility and temperature. People came into view and this time there were eight of them either sitting or kneeling in a circle on the sandy bottom about seven metres down. They had hollow metal objects on their backs which were new to Boji. Somehow these cylinders and the various parts and pipes attached to them must have made the humans independent of the surface for they were obviously breathing comfortably. Again their attention was centred on a single bottlenose dolphin, young and light in colour. She was drifting in and out of the circle, sometimes allowing herself to be touched, sometimes avoiding it. The water around this group was filled with a playfulness, a childlike joy devoid of fear, similar to what Boji had felt around Steven. Is this for me? he thought, and found himself drifting up again to see the location.

They were in a small cove, one of many inlets in a long coastline. The natural contours were broken up by numbers of buildings, square blocks of white, with many people lazing around them. More buildings were being put up, and they seemed to be swarming with busy humans and enveloped in machinery making dreadful noises. Boji was reminded of crowds of tiny reef fish jostling for territory on a small coral reef. He liked the water and the group of divers, but not the place.

Down again, and the sea became darker, a deep green this time with visibility around five metres. A large, adult male bottlenose dolphin, much older than Boji, swept by him. Intrigued, Boji followed, only to be overtaken by a swarm of boats of all shapes and sizes, inflatables, small fishing boats, and yachts. They all seemed to be chasing the dolphin he had just seen, who doubled back past him, clearly amused by the gleeful dance he was leading the humans, now all heading in the wrong direction.

He watched this dolphin slow down and swim into the shallows of a narrow, sandy beach where some children were playing. As he approached there were squeals of delight and welcome. The energy of the dolphin was expressed perfectly in the gentle, loving way he played with the young humans. Boji's heart was full. This was very close to his experience with Steven, containing, as it did, an innocence which seemed to disappear beneath heavier feelings as the humans grew into adulthood.

Where is this? he thought, and surfaced to take a look.

These waters were well protected. Temperate, neither cold nor tropical. He was just inside a narrow channel between two high headlands, one with a lighthouse on it. The channel opened out into a natural harbour which extended two or three kilometres back into the surrounding green fields. A small town, which no doubt supported all the boats, nestled against the waters at the back of the harbour.

He caught sight of dozens of humans bobbing about in the water, all with those full body suits on, and all intent on the dolphin whenever and wherever he blew. The body suits bothered him because he perceived they were a hindrance to his sonar. They seemed to contain nothing but tiny air bubbles trapped between two membranes of a different material. Those tiny air spaces gave him a kind of secondary echo to the higher frequencies of his sonar. It was those frequencies he relied on to know the inner physical state of whatever he was scanning, be it his prey, other dolphins, or humans.

Still he was drawn away, and this time swam beneath the surface for some distance, or so it seemed to him, before being presented with another scene. The sea was warm, clear and blue. The humans, when they appeared, did not need the body suits, indeed some of them, particularly the children, were entirely naked. He was attracted to them. He had never understood why people wore tiny strips of material in the water - they even had them on under the full body suits - strange!

There were at least ten humans in the water and they were all clearly at their ease in Boji's environment. Some were diving down wearing face masks and tubes, kicking the fins on their feet behind them. They didn't seem to be able to last long on the breath they were holding, and headed for the surface after only a brief exploration of whatever lay beneath them. Others were playing in the shallows.

What mystified Boji was the absence of a dolphin. Why am I being shown this, he thought, if these humans are not relating to a dolphin in any way?

He lifted to the surface.

He was in a lagoon about five hundred metres across and almost entirely enclosed. It was defined at one extreme by a rocky headland with angular ledges and sheer faces dropping into deep water. The profile of the land lost height and gave way to plush vegetation as it swept around to circle the calm waters of the lagoon. A sand beach started where the rocks of the headland surrendered to the softer landscape. Providing a gentle, curving cushion between land and sea, the sand stopped where a reef reached out and round toward the headland. A narrow, deep water channel some fifty metres across between reef and headland was the only break in the flattened circle of the lagoon's contours. This was the only beach on a small, fertile island. He felt the sea close all around. Humans in any great numbers were remote from this place. There were one or two single storey buildings which seemed to belong. They fitted snugly into the trees and upward sweep of the land behind the beach where it took over from the rocks of the headland.

Boji felt good watching this scenario. He wanted to make

contact with the swimmers, and for the first time wished he wasn't in the Dreamtime. This was a reality he could enjoy. The question came again - where was the dolphin? He had seen three other dolphins doing what he wanted to do. They were in three widely differing locations. Here was a fourth situation ripe for more human/dolphin interaction, and no dolphin in sight.

Then he got it - there is no dolphin to be seen here yet because I AM THE MISSING DOLPHIN!

His thoughts and feelings exploded. He was being shown the answer to his question 'Where am I to be?' A longer time in one place to develop the kind of familiarity and communication with others that he had experienced with Steven - and this is the place.

As soon as he had that realisation the scene began to fade. He wanted so much to stay there, yet even as the island disappeared and the sea darkened, he knew every detail of that vision was engraved on his mind. He would know that place the instant he saw it again.

The moon was again a fat crescent as Boji returned to the present in his existing reality. He filled and refilled his lungs three times very quickly. Leaping and tail-lobbing in a show of abundant energy, he thought now all I have to do is find the island!

TWENTY THREE

He found himself turning back automatically toward the stretch of continental coastline he had abandoned recently. So full was he of what he had seen and felt in the Dreamtime, that he had travelled for a kilometre or so before wondering if he was going in the right direction. He remembered that before he had arrived at the fourth and final place in his Dreamtime sequence, it had seemed as if he had swum a long way. It did not feel right to be heading back to the known when the unknown beckoned.

He hesitated for a moment, then turned round again and accelerated to fifteen knots knowing that, if necessary, he could keep up that speed for long periods. If an ocean had to be crossed then so be it!

Boji the Blue Dolphin felt again the excitement and the challenge of exploration and discovery within and without.

He had never travelled so far in a straight line. The deep water beneath him went on and on until he wondered if it would ever shelve up again. He beamed out ahead his deepest sonar frequencies which carried many kilometres. He had never been so one-pointed, maintaining his direction with a perception within him sensitive to the variations in the planet's magnetic field. He rested and fed whenever he felt those needs upon him, regardless of the hour of day or night.

Pleasant distractions appeared when he crossed shipping lanes, and he would indulge himself for a while, playing around large tankers and container ships.

Encounters with Sperm Whales reminded him of Mulata. He wondered if he would ever see the wise old bull again.

Not so pleasant was his meeting, at extreme sonar range, with a pod of Orcas coming toward him almost head on. That produced a diversion from his route and a very deep dive. Fortunately they didn't seem interested in a lone dolphin where they might otherwise have met a large school of pelagic dolphins.

Whatever happened, Boji always returned to the same course, covering sometimes two hundred kilometres a day. Time and distance became meaningless. A full month passed without him seeing any land.

Eventually, his sonar produced echoes of the sea bed coming up to meet him, and a profound sense of relief flooded through him. The open ocean had its attractions and challenges, but at that moment he was happy to leave deep water behind him for a while.

He slowed and spy-hopped, holding himself vertically in the water with his head above the surface.

As far as he could tell, he had come upon a string of islands sitting on a ridge rising from the ocean floor. His heart leapt. Could his destination be one of these islands? Certainly his directional pull had all but faded away, he had no wish to go beyond them.

The sun was low in the sky. It was the close of the thirty fifth day of his journey. Boji swam slowly toward the nearest of the islands. It was not much more than a large rock projecting from the sea. It was still a welcome sight to Boji. He moved in close to its leeward side, away from the ocean depths, and rested through the hours of night.

He resumed his quest at a leisurely pace the next morning. Life in the sea around these islands was abundant and rich in variety. He fed well as the sun rose in the sky, taking species of fish new to him after checking them out with his sonar.

He followed the ridge southward so he was constantly

over shallow waters between the islands. They were so different, and there was rarely more than a few kilometres from one to the next in the chain. Some he could see, even at a distance, were not the island he sought, and these he swam straight past. He covered nine the first day, ignoring four of them, swimming around five looking for the features which would correspond with his Dreamtime vision. One prompted close investigation. It had a lagoon of about the right size, and the reef defining one side, but no headland and the profile of the island was flat.

He moved on.

This was the pattern for the next four days. Boji began to wonder if he should leave this long chain of outcrops from the oceanic ridge and resume his original course. Yet the drive and determination which had carried him across the ocean were no longer present. That compulsion had been replaced by something softer, more accepting of his wanderings.

On the fifth day he met a large pod of Spotted Dolphins.

Smaller than Boji, they welcomed him readily enough and they gambolled together, the speckled skin of the adults flashing in the strong sunlight. He was drawn to the calves, their markings were distinct, attractive, and devoid of the spots which would develop in adulthood. The mothers however, were not so keen and told him with their body language and warning sounds not to get too close.

This encounter filled a whole day, so he lazed and waited for the dawn of the next day before resuming his search.

One or two of the larger islands showed signs of human habitation, but never as he had seen it in his vision.

Nine days into his island hopping, Boji moved away from yet another mass barely rising above the surface of the sea. The next island in the chain looked more promising.

102

He swam on for twenty minutes, blowing regularly, not sighting ahead of him. The occasional sonar blast and echoes kept him going in the right direction. When he slowed at last the island was only four hundred metres away. What he saw was a rocky shoreline dropping into the water without beaches, with land behind rising under a cloak of vegetation.

It's about the right size, he thought, as he started to swim round the island. A headland came into view providing a natural conclusion to the rocky shore he had seen so far. A tiny opening, then the end of a reef appeared as he moved faster now.

His heart was thumping as he headed for the gap. Is this the end of my search? The question filled his mind.

Drifting between rocks and reef, hugging the sea bed, his acoustic senses were creating image after image. All the underwater contours were right. The water stayed deep on his left where the rock faces came down sheer into the sea. In front of him and to his right, the sandy bottom shelved gently upward. Just inside the opening he blew and remained at the surface. He saw it all - as he had been allowed to see it before - in the Dreamtime. The curve of the beach, the buildings, the contours of the land, the reef .

In his exultation he felt huge, as big as an Orca. He leapt, tail-lobbed, and breached for several minutes.

He stopped abruptly. Where were the humans?

He spy hopped. As if in answer, two people were running down the beach in front of the buildings. They dashed into the water and swam toward him.

Boji submerged and drifted down, sending out close range sonar at the oncoming humans. As they dived down toward him he moved out to a distance at which he could sense them and, literally, sound them out. A couple, clearly, and without the slightest trace of fear. On the contrary, the water was filled with love, trust and welcome.

It was as if they had been expecting him.

This was the place he had been seeking, and these were the people. Only two of them for now. He knew there would be more.

Everything he had experienced in his life so far had led him to this moment.

He knew humankind were central to his destiny. He loved them unconditionally.

His spiral of learning had returned to another beginning.